GUARDING ERIN (SPECIAL FORCES: OPERATION ALPHA)

Guardian Seals: Book 3

NICOLE FLOCKTON

Dear Readers,

Welcome to the Special Forces: Operation Alpha Fan-Fiction world!

If you are new to this amazing world, in a nutshell the author wrote a story using one or more of my characters in it. Sometimes that character has a major role in the story, and other times they are only mentioned briefly. This is perfectly legal and allowable because they are going through Aces Press to publish the story.

This book is entirely the work of the author who wrote it. While I might have assisted with brainstorming and other ideas about which of my characters to use, I didn't have any part in the process or writing or editing the story.

I'm proud and excited that so many authors loved my characters enough that they wanted to write them into their own story. Thank you for supporting them, and me!

READ ON!
Xoxo
Susan Stoker

DEDICATION

This one's for you, Erin.

CHAPTER ONE

The engines of the military transport plane droned incessantly as Carlos "Italy" Porcelli studied his text messages. His nose ignored the combined smell of aviation fuel and six men who hadn't showered in days. The chatter of his teammates white noise to his ears. He knew he should be listening. Their last mission had gone to hell in a hand basket in a matter of seconds. If it wasn't for the quick thinking of their team lead, Brendan "Robot" Dean, there was every chance half the team, including him, would've returned home in pine boxes. A sobering thought at the best of times.

He went to stick his phone in his pocket but paused, reading the message again.

YOU NEED TO LET THIS GO, CARLOS. I'M FINE.

Problem was, he didn't believe for a single second Erin Furlan, his former high school sweetheart, was fine.

What the fuck was he doing?

Until a few months ago, life had been all about his SEAL brothers and having each other's backs as they went from covert mission to covert mission. Then a former teammate, Riley *Ash* Ashland, had needed the team's help. There'd been no hesitation in being there for him. Even though assisting Ash had required diving back into a past he'd left far behind—a past filled with decisions and actions he hated recalling. Plunging into his former life had put him in contact with the one person he'd buried so far deep in his psyche an archeologist would have trouble digging her up. Now his past was roaring to the forefront of his life again.

"Italy! Get your head out of your phone. You've been like a fucking teenage girl with the way you've had it glued to your hand the last hour. Somethin' you wanna tell us?" Robot's voice boomed around the interior of the plane.

"Get fucked," he responded and this time put his phone in his pocket, determined to do as Erin said—leave her the hell alone.

———

Hands braced against the white tile of his shower, the water cascaded down Carlos's back, washing away the grime of the last three weeks. They'd landed at base eight hours ago and had gone straight into a debriefing session with Commander Black, standard operating procedure on return. This time it was more unpleasant having to relive the moment when a few of them had faced their mortality. Even now, he recalled the sensation of Robot yanking hard on his vest pulling away from a deadly landmine.

Carlos slammed his fist against the tile, welcoming the stab of pain as it radiated through his bones. He should've been more aware of his surroundings. Should've seen the little silver prongs sticking up from the ground.

One second was all it had taken. A momentary lapse when his thoughts had drifted to Erin and it had almost caused him and his teammates irreparable damage.

He snapped the water off and stepped out, rubbing the towel over his body briskly. He thought about what he was going to do the rest of the day. Sleeping would be a good idea, but if he did that then he'd be awake all night. Even though he had the next two days off, it was better he got back into a decent sleep pattern as soon as he could.

Wandering into his bedroom and the distinctive ding of his phone signaling a text message filled the silence. His pulse rate kicked up a notch before he willed it to settle down. The message was probably from one of the guys, not from Erin. She'd made it pretty clear in her last message she didn't want anything to do with him. Best for both of them if they kept it that way.

"Shit," he muttered to himself as he pulled on boxer briefs. That was easier said than done. If he knew she was happy, he'd leave her alone. Problem was, his instincts screamed at him that something wasn't right.

He'd seen the way she flinched when he touched her arm. The way she wore jeans and a long-sleeved shirt when it was almost a hundred degrees with eighty percent humidity.

That trip to New York was now permanently etched into his memory. The two encounters he'd had with Erin played over and over in his mind when he let them, which was more often than he cared to admit.

A second ding signaled another message.

Two messages in quick succession, he couldn't ignore his phone. While he hoped it could be Erin, in all likelihood, it was probably Commander Black saying they had to ship out again. Regardless if they had time off or not, when the team was needed they jumped to action.

Carlos strode over to where his phone rested on his bedside table and tapped open his message app.

Relief washed over him when he saw the messages were from two of his teammates and not the Commander. He read Robot's message first.

WOLF AND HIS TEAM ARE IN VIRGINIA. GET YOUR ASSES DOWN TO MURPHY'S. WE ALL NEED A BEER.

The next message was from Tim "T-Rex" Exeter.

LAST ONE THERE BUYS THE FIRST ROUND.

Carlos rolled his eyes. T-Rex made everything a contest. He typed out a quick response.

I'M IN AND WE ALL KNOW IF ANYONE'S GONNA BE LATE IT'S GONNA BE YOU, T-REX. BRING PLENTY OF CASH.

He tossed his phone on his bed and finished dressing. Meeting the guys was the best way to get his mind off Erin, not to mention what they all needed after returning from a clusterfuck of a trip.

T he loud chatter hit him the second he walked into Murphy's, followed closely by the smell of stale beer and fried food. His stomach grumbled, reminding him he hadn't bothered to eat before he'd hit the shower at his apartment.

"Italy, over here."

He glanced at Ryan "Joker" Smith, who was seated adjacent to Robot, who sat next to the two newest members of the team, Greg "Cowboy" Robertson and Thomas "Red" Grant. Wolf and his team were there as well. He had to chuckle when he noticed T-Rex wasn't seated at the table.

Lifting his hand to let them know he'd seen them he weaved through the tables to where they sat against the side of the bar. The place was buzzing for a Wednesday afternoon. Guess the after-work crowd were enjoying a little hump day celebration.

He pulled out a chair and a bottle of beer sailed down the table in his direction. He took a long swallow. To the casual observer they would've looked like a weird group of men, all lined up with their backs to the wall. But if something happened, they'd be the first to see it and spring into action. The other patrons had no idea who was seated among them.

No introductions were needed, he recognized Wolf, Abe, Mozart, Cookie, Dude, and Benny. They'd all worked a couple of missions together. The other team had been a unit for a long time and had seen some crazy shit together.

He placed the bottle in front of him, the cool liquid settling in his stomach. "Fuck man, I needed that."

A murmured round of affirmatives greeted his comment. He studied everyone at the table. They all had that same tired look in their eyes, a weight to their shoulders.

"What brings you guys to town?"

"Passing through," Wolf said. "Not by choice. We'd all rather be back home."

Carlos nodded, knowing the whole team was married and a few of them had kids. "Unusual for you guys to be here."

"Yeah," Abe commented. "But you know how it is."

He didn't have to say anymore. Carlos understood exactly what he was getting at. "What time are you wheels up?"

"Ass crack of dawn, 05 00 hours," Wolf responded. "We arrive back a couple hours after dawn hits California."

Carlos lifted his beer in a silent salute "Ahh the quirks of different times zones. Hell of a long day."

"Tell me about it," Cookie said. "But at least we don't have to go through a debriefing. We did that here. We get to go home and lose ourselves in our women's arms and beds." He finished with a wink and his team-mates all clinked their bottles together.

What would it be like to have someone to come home to after each mission? It wasn't a thought that had crossed Carlos's mind often. He never allowed himself to float the idea of a serious relationship simply due to the nature of this job. The added risk of knowing that one misstep and he'd be leaving behind a wife and maybe a kid or two, never appealed. Hell, that had almost happened two days ago.

How these guys were able to go on mission after mission and not worry constantly about their families at home was a mystery to him. One thing he knew, he had no plans on asking them. He could imagine the shit his teammates would give him if asked relationship questions. Besides, he'd had his one and only true love relationship in his life. One he'd walked away from when he'd joined the service and left his old life behind.

His pocket vibrated as a shout went up from the men at the table. He looked up and saw T-Rex wandering toward them, a tray of beers in his hands and a waitress walking behind with another.

All thoughts of checking his phone forgotten as the beers landed on the scratched surface. The time had come to catch up with the guys. Just what he needed.

E rin's phone remained ominously quiet and she didn't dare check it in case Bryan saw her. Lost in her thoughts, she hadn't seen her ex-boyfriend standing on the outside stairs of the converted brownstone. If she'd been focused on her surroundings and not wondering what Carlos thought of her last message, she would've seen him sooner and, maybe, been able to change direction and not go home.

Although it wouldn't have lasted for long, she had to go home eventually. No doubt Bryan would've still been waiting for her. It was the exact type of asshole thing he'd do. Once again she asked herself how the hell she let herself fall in love with him.

No, that was wrong. It wasn't love. She'd been in a vulnerable situation after the death of a dear friend and Bryan had been there. A guy sitting at the bar who bought her a drink and tried to cheer her up.

What a mistake that had been to give him her number. Worse was actually continuing to see him after he'd grabbed her around the arms so tightly she had finger mark bruises on her flesh for days.

"I need a beer. Be a lamb and get me one," he sneered.

Over the past two months she'd allowed herself to believe he was finally out of her life. The mob family he'd been embroiled with had imploded after Giovanni Moretti had been taken into Federal custody, and had subsequently been murdered in prison. So many of

Giovanni's minions and runners had been taken into custody, Bryan included.

How the hell had he gotten out?

Erin shuddered at the thought of Bryan finding out the reason his *family* had disintegrated was because of her and their relationship. When she found out Bryan was a drug runner for the Moretti Mob she'd tried to walk away from him again. That time, she'd closeted herself away in her apartment and called in sick until the cuts and bruises had healed.

Anger at being a statistic of domestic abuse burned deep within her. She'd always told herself if the person she was involved with hurt her she'd walk away. But it was easier said than done. She'd known she wasn't in love with Bryan. The guy was a jerk, but with his connections she'd truly feared for her life. The Mob had ways of making people disappear without a trace.

Part of her had known someday something would happen and she'd get out from under his hold. And that something had turned up in the form of her former high school sweetheart. The man she'd given her heart, her first kiss, her virginity to, Carlos Porcelli. What a man he was now. He'd filled out his teenage body, and she had no doubt he was all muscle and strength.

When he asked her for her help in getting in touch with one of the guys he used to run around with, she'd been unable to say no, especially when she became aware if she helped Carlos she could potentially obtain her freedom. Problem was, Carlos was a Navy SEAL now. He saw things most people didn't see. When they'd been dating there'd been a streetwise edge about him. Over the years he'd honed it and looked even more dangerous than some of the guys Bryan hung out with.

He began asking questions, questions she didn't want to answer. Oh, how she wanted to tell him everything. He was a SEAL. He could protect her.

"Erin, why are you standing there like a fucking statue? I said I wanted a beer."

No more. Enough was enough.

"I don't have any beer. I want you to leave."

This bravado was something new for her. It had always been buried and she'd been too scared to use it. But now, after the past two months where her life had been her own and she'd been happy, she didn't want to go back into the abyss of hell that having Bryan in her life caused her.

Talking back to him, standing her ground was a big risk. Cowering to him was no longer what she wanted in her life.

"What did you say?" he spoke softly as he prowled toward her.

Her stomach churned. Wouldn't he just love it if she threw up all over him. That would show him weakness. He would feel triumphant knowing he still intimidated her.

"You heard me. I don't want anything to do with you anymore. I want you out of my house and my life."

He laughed. A horrid sound she'd never heard before. "Think again, *cara*. I'll always be in your life."

"I am not your *darling*. I never have been. Never will be. Now leave, Bryan or I'll call the cops."

"Call away, it won't do you any good. As far as the cops are concerned I'm squeaky clean."

What the hell? How could the cops think that about him? It was because he had a big mouth that she'd known she could help Carlos when he'd approached her about getting in touch with Rico. Bryan hadn't been discreet with some of his phone conversations so she knew he was involved in some bad shit. She took advantage of the opportunity to get more information when she'd walked into his study and found Bryan passed out next to a line of coke. Obviously, he'd been working while sampling the goods and the notebooks he made his notes in were open on his desk. Once she was certain he wasn't going to wake up she'd taken photos with her phone.

A ball of fear ballooned inside of her. Had he found out she'd taken photos? That it was because of her that Giovanni Moretti was arrested.

Immobilized by the thought, she couldn't move when Bryan raised his fist at her. She braced herself for the impact. The loud buzzing of her intercom penetrated the bubble of tension in her apartment.

A panicked look crossed Bryan's face, before it disappeared. "I was never here. But I'll be back, bitch."

Without giving her a chance to respond, he was out her front door. The buzzer sounded again and she had never been so grateful for that sound in all her life.

Whoever it was had saved her from a beating she may never have recovered from.

A yawn wracked Erin's body as she waited for her train. The person who'd rung her buzzer wanted the people who lived below her. They'd apologized for their mistake, but for Erin, she wanted to thank them profusely. Sleep had proved elusive though thanks to a combination of worry that Bryan might try and come back, and annoyance that Carlos hadn't responded to her message. She supposed she deserved not hearing from him. After all, her previous text had been for him to leave her alone.

Giving in to the urge, she pulled her phone out from her pocket—still no response. The rumble of the train echoed through the station. The mass of people on the platform surged toward the edge. With a screech of brakes, the train stopped and the doors slid open. Pushing through the crowd, she located a rare seat and sat down. She held her breath as an overpowering musk scent assailed her senses. What did the guy she sat next to do? Take a bath in his cologne. It was going to be a long journey.

Her phone buzzed and her heart leaped in her throat. When she saw it was from her girlfriend, Antonia, a little stab of disappointment replaced the hope that it was Carlos who contacted her.

HEY, WE'RE ALL MEETING FOR DINNER TONIGHT AT FREDRICO'S. YOU IN?

It had been a while since she'd met up with her friends. A girl's night could be exactly what she needed.

COUNT ME IN. TIME?

AWESOME, DOES 6.00 WORK FOR YOU?

As general manager of Hotel Coquillage her work hours were pretty standard. It wasn't a guarantee that anything could happen at any given time that could extend her hours. Her girlfriends knew that and didn't mind if she wasn't always on time.

BARRING ANY CRAZY ISSUES, I'LL BE THERE. ORDER ME A G&T.

Antonia responded with a thumbs up and kissy face emoji. A chuckle escaped Erin. This was just what she needed to put the events from the previous evening behind her.

The thought of Bryan somehow being able to break into her apartment while she was at work sent chills up her spine. It still freaked her out that he'd been standing outside of her building last night. His presence unexpected and, definitely, unwelcome.

Her mind turned to Carlos and wished he was close by. Such a stupid thought, there wasn't anything he could do, but part of her wanted to unload all her issues on him. Being a SEAL his first instinct would be protect and guard those around him.

What would it hurt if she sent him another message? She had no idea where he was based or if he was even in the States. Maybe that was why he hadn't responded to her text.

Before she thought about it for too much longer she opened the message thread and began typing.

HEY, I NEED SOME HE...

She had no idea what to say. Maybe it would be best if she didn't send him one after all. It would be safer for him not to be anywhere near her. With Bryan back in the picture, there was no telling if any of his other friends were also out. Or he might have tried to get himself in good with another mob family. With the information he had about the Moretti Mob's drug connections, Bryan would be a valuable addition to any family.

Erin snorted quietly at that thought. Bryan had enough arrogance in him to think he could start his own drug running business. Yes, that was more like what he'd do, which made staying away from him even more imperative. If his plan was to start his own business he had to look the part, including a beautiful woman hanging off his arm. Nope, not the job she wanted at all. He could find some other bunny for that role.

The train screeched to a halt at her stop. She shoved the phone in her purse, determined to forget about Bryan and Carlos.

CHAPTER TWO

Carlos's head pounded and he regretted that last beer. What had they been thinking? He imagined his wasn't the only sore head in the group. His mouth was as dry as sandpaper. He knew if he breathed on anyone, it would smell like he'd licked the bottom of an ashtray, and he didn't even smoke. The days of drinking like he had in his early twenties were over.

He rolled over preparing to catch a few more z's as his phone chimed with an incoming message.

Ignore it.

Tempting, but he couldn't. It'd been bad enough last night when Robot called him a *girl* every time he went to pull the damn thing out of his pocket. Robot had assured him, and the rest of his team, that the Commander wouldn't be contacting them with fresh orders. Carlos noticed his team lead hadn't given the guys on the other team a hard time when they checked their phones. Then again, they were a separate team, *and* were all married.

Sitting up he reached across to grab his phone off his bedside table, his head swimming at the movement. His stomach did a couple of somersaults before it settled down. Keying in the passcode, he got comfortable and opened his message app.

His blood turned cold and the fog of his heavy night dissipated as he read the most recent message from Erin.

HEY, I NEED SOME HE…

What the hell?

Carlos read the message from the previous evening. The one he'd been forced to ignore.

HEY THERE CARLOS, MY LAST MESSAGE WAS A LITTLE HARSH. IT WASN'T MEANT TO BE. NEXT TIME YOU'RE IN NEW YORK CALL ME. IT WAS GOOD TO SEE YOU AGAIN.

Okay, so that message wasn't ominous so why did he think the one from a few minutes ago was. Clearly it had been sent before she'd finished typing it. Maybe it was nothing at all. Yet he couldn't ignore the little itch in the middle of his left palm, his warning sign something wasn't right. Other guys had itches on the back of their neck or a feeling in their gut. Not one person made fun of the other person's *warning signs*, because nine times out of ten, those signs saved each other's lives.

There was only one way to find out if everything was okay with Erin, and that was to call her. He drummed his fingers on his thigh as he waited for the call to connect.

Hi, you've called Erin. I'm unable to take your call now, but leave me a message. Thanks.

No, he didn't want to leave a message. What he wanted to do was call her to make sure she was okay.

Thumbing through his contacts he pulled up Ash's number. His former SEAL team member lived in New York, plus he ran a security/PI firm. No doubt he had some computer program that would be able to determine if Erin was in trouble or not.

"Riley Ashford."

"Ash, it's Italy."

"Hey, man, what's up?"

He drummed his fingers on the sheets. "I need you to check up on something if you can."

"Sure, what do you need?"

Carlos hadn't let Ash know how he'd obtained the information they'd used to help free Maria from her family's clutches. How hard it had been to think about seeing the people from his former life. The one he'd lived before he'd joined the Navy. He hadn't seen any of the old gang, because Erin had said she could help him more than Rico could. He'd been torn in two by her offer. If he'd seen Rico again, it would've dredged up memories of the shitty things he'd done and the hole he'd fallen into as a teenager. But talking to Erin, seeing her again, brought back feelings he'd denied himself over the last sixteen years. In the end, seeing Erin was the lesser of the two evils. Or so he'd thought at the time.

"Are you able to tap into someone's location using their cell phone?"

"I can," Ash paused. "Why?"

"I got a message from a friend. I want to make sure she's okay."

"Why don't you call her?"

"I did, and it went straight to voicemail."

"What's the issue? Maybe they were busy or out of cell service. There are still cell phone black holes in Manhattan."

For a second, Carlos pondered whether making this call was the most sensible thing he'd done. All he wanted Ash to say was, *sure, give me the number and I'll get back to you.*

Ash interrupted his thoughts. "I'm sensing there's more you're not telling me, Italy."

Time to come clean. He could trust Ash with the information he was about to relay. He may have left the service, but the brotherhood code never died between team members.

"The information I got for you which helped bring down the Moretti mob was from a former girlfriend. I think she's in trouble."

"Why do you think that? Is she part of a mob family? Is she dangerous?" Ash fired off the questions in quick succession, his tone serious. Carlos could understand him asking if Erin was dangerous. The last thing Ash would want to do would be to put his girl-friend, Maria, in danger again. Put her back in the line of sight of the mob families of New York. He'd just gotten her away from all that danger. They both deserved to be able to live their lives without the specter of possible threats from the mob.

"Erin has no connection to any mob family. She's about as dangerous a new born baby."

"If she has no connection to any of the families still active in New York, how did she get the information she did? You don't get that type of intel without having some sort of insider knowledge of the workings of the organization."

Carlos couldn't argue with Ash. Everything he said was correct. He and Erin had grown up in the same neighborhood. He was the one who'd gotten caught up with a mob family. He thought he'd kept it hidden from Erin when they'd been dating, perhaps he'd been wrong and she'd known what he'd done when he was younger.

Of course, things could've changed in the last sixteen years. He hadn't questioned how she got the information, had just been grateful to have it in his hands. Plus, he knew the longer he was around Erin, the harder it would be to walk away. Seeing her again had him remembering everything they'd shared together. How she'd felt in his arms, her lips against his. The last thing he needed in his life was a walk down memory lane. Being alone was the best thing for him considering his career.

"Italy? Talk to me."

"Look, I can't guarantee she's not involved with the mob, but my left palm is itching, and it only itches when something isn't right. I've learned to trust this feeling over the years."

"Fine." Ash sighed heavily. "How about I put this in Tex's hands. He has more ways of finding information than I do. If she's integrated into a family, he'll discover it."

Carlos knew about Tex. The former SEAL had been instrumental in their takedown of the Moretti Mob. The guy had access to connections that even some of the top military personnel didn't have. "I didn't think it was necessary to bother Tex, but perhaps it would be for the best."

"I'll call him and get back to you. What are you going to do in the meantime?"

A plan of action began to form in his mind. "Talk to the Commander about getting some personal leave and take a trip to Manhattan."

"You can bunk with us if you like," Ash offered.

"Thanks, man. I'll text you when I get there."

"Later."

Carlos disconnected and threw the covers back. He strode to his kitchen and grabbed a bottle of water and a couple of aspirin. If he had a trip to make, he was going to make it without his head throbbing.

C arlos placed his bag in Ash's spare room. He'd been able to get an early afternoon flight out of Virginia. His stomach grumbled, reminding him he hadn't eaten all day. Over the years, the face of Manhattan had changed, but one thing remained the same—you could always find a good pizza pie anywhere.

His jacket pocket vibrated, pulling it out. Tex's name flashed on the screen. Strange, he didn't have Tex's number in his contacts. The guy wasn't someone he had any reason to contact on a regular basis. Well, that is until now.

"Hello?"

"Hi, Italy, this is Tex."

"Yeah, I saw your name pop up, which is, hmm, interesting."

Tex chuckled, but didn't respond to his comment. "I've got information on Erin Furlan. Ash said you wanted it."

"Yeah, I've got a feeling something's not right with her."

"Good call. The last two years haven't been the best for her. She got herself tangled up with a runner from the Moretti Mob, Bryan Tosconi."

Carlos's heart sank. He hadn't wanted to believe Erin was involved with the family.

"Fuck. No wonder she was able to get that information."

"Yeah, but the guy's a real piece of work."

He tensed at the disgusted tone in Tex's voice. "What do you mean by that?"

"He talks more with his fists than his mouth."

Carlos swore again. "Tell me he didn't put her in the

hospital?" He hadn't wanted to think that Erin was being hurt, but everything started falling into place in his mind. The way she'd flinched when he'd touched her the last time he'd seen her. Her reluctance to talk to him when he questioned her. Not to mention the text telling him to let it go. Her actions were typical of a person who denied their boyfriend or husband was harming them.

"There are no hospital records, but that doesn't necessarily mean anything. Only anomaly I could find was six months ago, she took a week off work."

"How is that unusual? She could've just been sick. Or gone away," he commented.

"You're right, but if she was sick, there would've been record of a doctor's visit. There's no record of her leaving the state. Her bank account wasn't touched for the week. The guy has a violent background. I'm not one to jump to conclusions, but things don't add up."

Anger pulsed through Carlos. "Did the Feds put that fucker away?" The piece of scum needed to be off the streets and out of Erin's life for good.

"They did," Tex paused, and he braced himself for what the man was about to say next. "But he made bail the other day."

"What? How is that possible? If Erin got the information from him, how come they didn't throw the book at him?"

"Seems the guy's got good lawyers. Plus, they couldn't find any concrete evidence he was deeply involved in the organization's business."

"That's fucking bullshit. Unless…"

"No, don't go there, Italy. She's not involved with any family."

"How can you be so sure?"

Tex sighed. "Because she doesn't live the life of a person who is heavily tangled up in the drug industry. She's the General Manger of a Manhattan boutique hotel. She lives on the third story of a Brownstone. Not flashy. Takes public transport. Pays off her credit cards each month."

He trusted what Tex was telling him to be the truth. Now he wanted to see Erin. He had to make sure for himself that she was okay. "Can you send me everything you've got, Tex?"

"It's already on its way to you. By the way, she's having dinner with her girlfriends at Fredrico's tonight. They're meeting up at six."

It was on the tip of his tongue to ask how Tex knew that information, but figured it was best not to question his methods. Just take the information and run with it. "Right. Thanks for everything, Tex. I appreciate it."

"Not a problem, man, I'm always here. You have my number now."

Carlos chuckled. "Yes, I do."

The line disconnected and Carlos checked his email to see that Tex had kept his word and emailed the report. He would study it later. Right now he needed to go see Erin. It could be the worst idea he had, but he didn't care. If that scum Bryan was back on the streets, he would guard Erin and keep her safe, while trying to find a way to get Bryan put away for good.

———

E xhaustion bit at her heels. It had been a shit of a day. A computer software problem had all their reservations jumbled up tighter than a pair of stockings in a washing machine. The last thing she wanted to do was go to dinner, but she really needed a girl's night.

She turned the light off and closed her office door. At the end of each day a sense of pride filled her with all she'd accomplished in the past four years. Hard work and determination had gotten her to the position of General Manager quicker than she ever imagined possible.

Before she left, she stopped at the registration desk. "If any issues crop up overnight, call me. No matter what the time."

The clerk smiled. "Certainly, Erin. Hopefully, I won't have to. Have a good night."

"Thanks." Secretly, Erin prayed her phone wouldn't ring. After dinner she planned to go home and fall into bed. Between the stress of Bryan turning up in her life again, and today's work drama, a solid eight hours of sleep sounded like an unreachable dream.

She skipped down the stairs, glad to be outside and absorbed everything that made New York, New York. The sounds of taxi drivers sitting on their horns, the aroma coming from the hotdog stand on the corner, the flow of people streaming out of the subway stations.

"Hello, Erin."

Shocked at hearing Carlos's voice, her foot slipped and she missed the bottom step. Instead of finding herself kissing the sidewalk, warm, strong arms closed around her. Without thinking, she laid her head on Carlos's chest. She breathed deeply and the aroma of hotdogs was replaced with a tangy citrus smell that was intoxicating. She inhaled again.

He chuckled. "Did you just smell me?"

Erin came to her senses and pulled away from him. Surprise made way for embarrassment. "What are you doing here?"

If she thought her terseness would put him off, she was living in a fantasy world. Instead of putting distance between them, he grabbed her hand again.

"I got your text message and I was worried."

"What text message?" Confusion colored her thoughts. She knew she'd sent him a text last night, but she hadn't asked him to travel up to New York to see her. She expected him to call.

His hand went to his pocket and pulled out the phone, all the while he maintained his hold on her. Her skin sizzled from the connection, drawing her back to the first time they'd kissed when they'd been sixteen. At the time, she'd thought her reaction to his touches and kisses had been because he was her first boyfriend. A crush that had turned into juvenile love. Now she had to wonder.

After the first couple of dates with Bryan, her body had never flared to life like hers was doing right now. They were only holding hands for goodness sake.

"This message." A phone was shoved under her nose.

"I didn't send ..." She re-read the message and then it hit her. This was the message she'd started to send to him while on the subway and then she'd had second thoughts. "I, um, I didn't mean to send it to you."

"Right. Who were you sending it to?"

She could fabricate that she was sending it to a friend. Somehow she didn't think he would buy it. "You."

"But?"

"Well, you didn't respond to my message last night and then I didn't know what to say."

Everything she'd told him was the truth. The only problem was she still didn't know what to say to him. For a brief second on the train she'd wanted to ask him for his help with Bryan. She'd helped him, he could help her. But could she ask that of him though?

"I was out last night, and didn't see your message until I checked my phone this morning."

"Uh huh. Well," she looked at their connected hands and then at the crowd bustling around them. "I've got plans, so I'd better get going. Good seeing you, Carlos."

She went to pull her hand out of his grip, but he tightened his hold on her.

"What's going on, E? And don't tell me nothing. I know you. I can see the tension in you."

Anger rippled through her and she yanked her hand out of his grip. "You don't know me at all now. You were the one who walked away from me. From *us*. And yes, I'm tense. After the shit day I had, you'd be tense as well. Now, if you'll excuse me I've got places to be. Real friends to catch up with. Goodbye, Carlos."

With that, she tossed her dark hair over her shoulder and strode down the sidewalk, weaving in out of the crowd. She may have wanted to connect with him this morning, but he'd blown that out the window with his arrogant assumption that he knew her. He knew nothing about her now. He'd forfeited that right when he'd left her sixteen years ago. It would be better for them both if he stayed away.

CHAPTER THREE

The rush-hour crowd swallowed Erin as Carlos stood there rooted to the spot as though the concrete had set around his feet.

She blew him off? She was angry *at* him? Okay so maybe he deserved her anger. Since 9/11, enlisting had been the only thing on his mind. It had fired him up to finish his final year of high school with the best grades possible, even while doing shitty things for the mob. He'd hit the local Navy office to enlist before the ink had dried on his graduation certificate. He'd known that, while the mob was a corrupt organization, they usually only killed those who betrayed them.

What Erin wasn't aware of was, Carlos did know what was going on in her life at the moment. Whether she believed it or not, she was in danger. With asshole Bryan out on the streets, and the fact he'd already hurt Erin on more than one occasion, Carlos had no intention of letting that happen to her.

"Get out of the way, jerk." A harried businessman brushed past him, forcing him into action.

Carlos walked in the direction Erin had departed. He pulled out his phone and typed in the name of the restaurant in his maps app. He studied the screen and continued on his way. His plan would be to watch, make sure nothing happened to her. No way would he encroach on her time with her girlfriends. With his skills, he planned to blend into the crowd without being noticed. Although, maybe hiding in plain sight of her was a better way to go.

He reached *Frederico's* and opened the door. His stomach grumbled as the scents of tomatoes, garlic and pizza crust floated through the air. Yeah, he could totally go for a thick New York crust works pizza.

He scanned the crowd and located Erin in a matter of seconds. She was with three other women. They were seated at a table in the middle of the room, laughing and clinking shot glasses together before downing them.

"Do you have a reservation, sir?"

Carlos turned his attention to the hostess and smiled. "No, I don't."

"How many in your party?"

He glanced again over to where Erin and her friends sat. If she looked in the direction of the front door she'd see him. "There's only me."

"Okay, let me see what I can do." The young woman studied the computer screen in front of her for a few moments before looking back at him. "I'm afraid it will be a forty-minute wait for a table. If you would like to, you can sit at the bar. We offer full menu service there as well."

Sitting at the bar with his back to room had his skin crawling. He hated being in a vulnerable position like that. Anyone could spring a surprise attack on him. As he wanted to keep an eye on Erin, he would have to suck it up. Maybe he could find a stool that gave him an optimum view of the room.

"The bar's fine."

"Excellent, Sam will show you the way."

Five minutes later, Carlos had an ice-cold beer in front of him and had found a spot where he had views of the exit, the kitchen and Erin's table. As he lifted his beer he observed Erin and her interaction with her friends. The brunette sitting next to her looked vaguely familiar. Their heads were close together and they appeared to be having a deep conversation. Not an easy thing to do in a loud restaurant. The other two women present were laughing at something and he spied the flash of diamonds on their left hands indicating they were married.

A waiter arrived at their table with a tray full of steaming food, Erin shifted back to allow him to place their dishes in front of her. She turned her head toward the bar. Carlos may have angled himself so he had an unobstructed view of her. He wasn't sure the same could be said for her.

Her eyes widened and then narrowed. The luscious lips he'd devoured as a teenager firmed into a thin line.

Busted.

He wasn't exactly disappointed that she'd spotted him. He raised his beer bottle in her direction before going back to appearing like he was relaxed. SEALs never fully relaxed. In their job, relaxing meant the difference between life and death.

He smelled her before he heard her. Even after a full day at work, he could still discern the scent of wildflowers coming from her in a crowded restaurant.

"What are you doing here?" she demanded.

He shrugged. "Having a beer and a pizza. I've missed New York pizzas."

"Really? How convenient you happen to be at the same place I'm having dinner with my girlfriends."

He quickly changed the way he sat so he trapped her between his legs. "A happy coincidence for sure."

Her body stiffened at the contact of his thighs against hers. "That's a bullshit line if I've ever heard one. How about you tell me the real reason why you're here?"

He leaned forward and waited for her to copy his action. A breath huffed out of her as she closed the distance. He kept his voice low so only Erin could here what he was about to say. "I know everything's not *fine* with you. So yeah, here I am keeping an eye on you."

Anger highlighted the sparks of gold in her hazel eyes. He'd seen that look a few times when they'd been dating. She had a fiery Italian temper. Sometimes he'd deliberately made her mad just so he could see the fire and then kiss her senseless. Nothing like anger kisses to get the blood boiling. Even now his dick twitched against the seam of his jeans. It had been a long time since he'd been with a woman. A long, *long*, time since he'd been with Erin. But he'd never forgotten their encounters. No woman got him off as quickly as Erin had done with her mouth.

"Ugh. You are so infuriating." The words burst out of her, as though she'd read where his thoughts had been heading. Before he could respond, she'd whirled around and stomped back to the table. Her slim skirt cupped her ass nicely. As a teenager she'd been perfectly proportioned. Now as an adult, her curves had grown more luscious and he'd like nothing better than to let himself fall into her orbit again.

The arrival of his pizza pulled him from his lustful thoughts. While he ate, he kept up his surveillance of the room and Erin's table. If Bryan walked in, he would know. He hadn't had a chance to have a good look at the information Tex had sent him. He'd given it a cursory glance and had planned to study it further on the plane, but he'd taken a good look at the guy's picture. Unfortunately, his head still pounded from the night before, so he'd slept most of the flight instead.

An hour later, Erin and her friends were hugging each other goodbye. He'd been the subject of many glares from the occupants of the table, so he wasn't surprised when the girl who'd been sitting next to Erin walked up to him.

"Carlos Porcelli, it's been a while."

No matter how casual or friendly her tone might seem to anyone watching them, Carlos knew it was the exact opposite. Up close, the woman seemed even more familiar to him. He racked his brain, flitting through the women he'd known over the years. It wasn't a huge number, but he was able to cross off, with certainty, that she wasn't on his taken-to-bed list.

He was about to admit defeat when her name popped into his head. *Antonia*. Erin's best friend from high school. "Antonia Rocca. Damn, you're right it has been a while. How are you?"

She crossed her arms, the action lifting her breasts. The sight of her cleavage didn't get his blood racing like the thought of an angry Erin did. "I'm fine. But I'm not happy that you're back in town."

He sat up a little straighter. Okay, if he wanted to get out of here alive, it looked like he'd need to watch his words very carefully. "Why?"

She shook her head in disbelief, as if he should know why she was unhappy she was standing in front of him. "You're bad news. I know all about your association with the Faloni Family. You may be a SEAL now, but you can't change your past."

If she knew about his time with the mob, did that mean he'd been naïve in thinking Erin didn't? The mob was all around their neighborhood. Hell, they recruited kids at the local middle school to be part of their crew. That was how he'd gotten sucked into it. His family needed the money, and it was a sure fire way to earn good cash. When he'd taken the step back into his former life to get information for Ash, he'd been aware it had the potential to put him back on the radar with some of the old crew. The ones who hadn't been happy with his decision to bail on them all those years ago, even if it was for a noble cause like joining the military. To them it was still a betrayal, leaving the family who had done so much for him. Hence why he'd jumped when Erin had said she could help him. He shouldn't have jumped. He should've stuck to his guns. But if he hadn't he wouldn't be able to give Erin the protection she needed.

With the resolve that had gotten him through BUD/s training, he pushed the memories to the farthest part of his mind. "My past is just that. The past. I'm not here to hurt Erin. I'm here to protect her."

Antonia scoffed. "You've already hurt her once. I'm watching you so you don't hurt her again."

Without giving him a chance to respond, she turned on her heel and marched through the restaurant. Erin stood watching him. If she knew what Antonia had said to him, she gave no indication.

As the quartet walked out of the restaurant, Carlos let Antonia's words sink into his consciousness.

You've already hurt her once.

Was she referring to when he'd left after graduation? Erin had known he was going to enlist. In fact, she'd encouraged him to do it. They'd spent the night before graduation together. He recalled their lovemaking. It had been sweet and sexy. It had also been their goodbye. They were following different career paths. He hadn't made her any promises about a future together and she hadn't made any to him. Had she been hoping he'd ask her to join him after he finished his basic training? No, the idea was ridiculous. He knew she'd wanted to get her degree. If she'd followed him around, that would never have happened.

They had emailed each other for a couple of months, in the beginning. Then he'd gotten busy with training and she with her college degree. He'd never forgotten her, though. She'd been his first love.

His only love.

Wolf's team may have all found women to spend the rest of their lives with while they were still on active duty. He had no plans on putting a woman he loved through the pain of never knowing whether he would return from a mission alive, injured, or in a pine box.

"Sir? Can I get you anything else?"

The bartender intruded his thoughts. Carlos looked up at the man. "Uh no." He grabbed a wad of bills from his wallet and threw them on the bar. "Thanks."

Getting caught up in his thoughts, he had no idea how long it had been since Erin and her friends had walked out the door. From the quick look he'd given Tex's report, Carlos knew she lived in Queens. Would she have taken an Uber, or would she have taken the subway? Or maybe even a cab. He hoped she hadn't decided to ride the subway. Shady characters rode the trains late in the evening. The type of characters that would do drug deals. Surely Antonia wouldn't have let her do that?

Whichever way she got herself home, he planned to make sure she'd got there safely. Hailing a passing cab, he climbed in when it stopped and rattled off Erin's address. As the car weaved through the night heading toward his destination, Carlos drummed his fingers on his thigh, giving the driver one syllable answers to the questions he asked.

All he wanted to do was to get to Erin to make sure she was safe in her apartment. He mentally cursed Antonia for pulling him from the present and tossing him into the past. What he and Erin had shared probably wouldn't have lasted the distance, no matter how much they'd hoped it would. If he hadn't gone into the Navy, he'd have been sucked further into the vortex of mob life. He'd resisted the temptation of drugs as a teenager, something a few of the other guys hadn't been able to ignore. Who was to say that, eventually, he wouldn't have succumbed to the power of the white powder the Forlani family was known for? Or been arrested and be incarcerated, right now. Dragging Erin into that sort of life wasn't what he had wanted for her. She'd deserved so much better and with the job she had, he knew if they'd stayed together, she wouldn't have the career she had now.

The cab pulled to a stop a couple houses down from Erin's brownstone. He swiped his credit card and paid the fare. As the car took off into the night, the tail-lights disappearing around the corner, he contemplated the best way of finding out if Erin was safe inside.

He knew she lived on the third floor. The windows facing the street were dark, but that didn't mean there weren't lights on at the back half of the building. The street wasn't a busy one. Then again it was almost midnight.

Carlos slipped into the shadows and tried to see if there was a way he could get to the back of her building. As the long, black shadows enveloped him into their dark embrace, another vehicle pulled to a stop.

The sound of feminine laughter reached his ears. *Erin.* "Night, Antonia. You have no idea how much I needed this tonight."

He didn't catch what Antonia's response was but whatever she said, made Erin giggle again. A sound he hadn't heard in a very long time. He was pleased she was happier now and his appearance at the restaurant hadn't totally ruined her evening.

The door slammed shut and the car took off. The clip clop of her shoes echoed around the street. He would watch her enter the building, wait for the lights to go on and then leave, content with the knowledge she was safe for the night.

"Hey, bitch, where have you been? I've been waiting for fucking hours for you." The words shattered the quiet. Carlos crouched down and crept toward the front of the brownstone, making sure he didn't make a sound to alert the others of his presence.

"Bryan, what are you doing here?"

Shit. He hadn't wanted to believe it could be the other man, but who else would be that rude to her?

"I told you I'd be back. And I want what's mine."

Coldness enveloped him at Bryan's threat. No way was that fucker going to lay a hand on Erin. Not on his watch.

Stamping his feet on the pavement, he walked into the glow of the streetlight. "Okay, honey, you were right the subway is slower than the cab." He walked quickly toward Erin and bound up the stairs where she appeared to be rooted to the spot.

He slipped his arm around her waist and moved Erin so he stood in front of her. He willed her not to give Bryan any indication that she didn't welcome his touch.

"Who the fuck are you?" Bryan asked. "And where did you come from?"

From the building's porch light, Carlos recognized the glassiness in the other man's eyes. He was so high he probably thought he could fly. He thanked God he had managed to beat Erin home. He didn't want to think about what might have happened if he hadn't been there.

"Not that it's any of your business, but I'm Erin's boyfriend."

Erin sputtered behind him and he gave her waist a squeeze, a silent message to let him deal with this. Her breath hissed out, but she relaxed a fraction against him.

"That's bullshit. I know she doesn't have a boyfriend. This is the first time I've seen you around here. And I know you didn't get out of the car with her."

"What the hell, Bryan? You've been watching me?"

Bryan didn't seem to care that Carlos was standing on the stoop with them. The other man leaned in. "Yeah, I've been watching you. I know you've got something of mine. And I plan to get it."

Enough was enough. Carlos let go of Erin, and shifted her so she was fully behind him. He then pulled himself up straighter and eyeballed the son of a bitch. "Listen here, fucker. You come anywhere near Erin and you'll answer to me. *Capisce?*"

They glared at each other. Oh man, how Carlos wished Bryan would come at him. He'd like nothing better than to teach the asshole a lesson. But like all bullies when confronted, Bryan was the first to look away.

He took one step backward, then another. "You don't scare me. You'd better watch your back, cause I'll be watching you, too." He finished with giving them the bird before stomping down the stairs and weaved his way into the middle of the street.

"With any luck he'll get hit by a random car," Erin muttered.

Carlos laughed at her comment. "Bastard wouldn't be so lucky. Now, let's get you inside. I want to check your apartment."

"I don't think so. I'm still mad at you for turning up at the restaurant."

"I told you that was a happy coincidence."

Erin pushed him out of the way as she made her way to the door. "Oh please, do me the courtesy of not lying.

Admit it, Carlos, you're following me. If you weren't, you wouldn't be standing here."

"And wasn't it lucky I was? If I hadn't been here, who knows what danger you would be in. When are you going to concede that you're not fine, Erin? That you're not safe."

CHAPTER FOUR

Still shaken up by Bryan's appearance again on her doorstep, not to mention Carlos turning up like some knight in shining armor, all Erin wanted to do was get upstairs to her apartment and crash on her bed. A 6.00 a.m. call came around mighty quickly when it was after midnight.

Damn Carlos and all his sexy SEALness. No way was she going to admit the relief that poured through her when he burst out of the shadows. Fear had clutched her so tightly when Bryan had threatened her she wasn't sure she could've said anything that would've turned her ex-boyfriend away.

"Don't deny it, Erin. Don't deny you need guarding."

Tiredness seeped through her cells. Would it be so terrible to do what he said and admit her life was becoming a shambles? Would it be so bad to have Carlos check out her apartment?

"Will you leave if I say yes?"

"Define leave."

"Seriously? It's after midnight, Carlos. I told you I had a shit day. The buzz I had from hanging with my girls is gone. The last thing I want to do is get into some sort of in depth discussion about the word *leave*."

His warm hand gripped her waist and he nudged her forward. Resistance was useless. The minutes he'd held her against him while he'd been protecting her from Bryan had been blissful. She'd always loved being held by him. No man had ever given her the same sense of security as Carlos gave her. Even now, after all those years they'd been apart, one touch and her body remembered.

The urge to fight seeped out of her and her shoulders dropped. "Fine. You can come upstairs. But I want you to leave when you've done what you want to do."

"We'll see."

Reaching out to the keypad she put in the code and the door buzzed open. The welcoming atmosphere of the building's entry hall enveloped her. The comforting scent of the rose potpourri that Mrs. Wilson, who lived in the ground floor apartment, replaced every day filled the space. The muted golden light cast from the crystal chandelier gave the open area a welcoming feel, which was one of the main reasons why she'd chosen this place to live.

Carlos whistled. "Impressive entry."

"I know. I love it." Once she saw it she knew she didn't want to live anywhere else. She made her way to the elevator, conscious of Carlos following her. The times she'd glanced over her shoulder at the restaurant, she'd observed the way Carlos continually scanned the room, almost like he expected danger to pop up at any second. She supposed in his job he would have to constantly be on high alert.

The doors parted and she stepped into the small cart. Carlos followed and filled the space with his broad shoulders and six-foot plus frame. Before tonight she'd always thought the elevator was cute in its smallness. Now she wished it was triple the size.

"Cozy."

"Mmmhmm." His scent filled the small space, such an addictive smell. The combination of the man and his cologne, spicy and tangy, made her want to taste his neck.

Thankfully, she was saved from her folly by the car stopping and the doors opening on her floor. Carlos laid an arm across the door to hold it open. He needn't have bothered. She had no plans to hang around in the confined space.

Her key slid into the lock and before she turned it, his hand closed over hers. "Let me."

She relinquished her hold on the small metal object and took a step back, right into his hard chest. For a second she allowed herself to relax into him. With his leather jacket open, heat emanated through the thin fabric of his shirt. He'd always been warm. On cold winter's days he would pull her gloves off and rub his hands over hers. Within seconds she was warm and he'd slip her gloves back on. The heat never lasted long, but for the short time it did she savored it.

"Wait here," he said in a low voice.

"Right."

He turned the key and eased the door open. There was no welcoming light because she'd already left for the day when Antonia had contacted her for dinner. If she knew she had after work plans, she normally left a light on.

She made a move to walk into the apartment behind Carlos, but he held up a hand halting her. Dread began to climb through her. She'd always thought her building was safe, believed the chance of anyone breaking in to be slim. Mrs. Wilson on the ground floor was always watching the comings and goings of people entering. If Bryan had wanted to break into her place, wouldn't he have done it last night instead of waiting outside for her to return home? Like he did again tonight.

"It's all clear you can come in now."

Erin walked into her darkened apartment and flicked the hallway light on. She blinked rapidly at the brightness. "How the hell could you tell my apartment's fine if you didn't turn the lights on?"

He shrugged casually. "I don't need lights."

Realization struck. "Ahh SEAL night vision?"

"Yeah something like that."

While she'd been aware of Carlos's career choice, she never allowed herself to really think about what he did. The danger he faced every day and night.

"Is it always bad?" she asked.

His shoulders tensed and his face blanked of any emotion. "It's late. I thought you were tired."

Okay, then, no comment. She shouldn't be surprised. The things he'd seen over the years were probably worse than she could ever imagine.

A yawn ripped through her. "Yeah, I'm exhausted. Thanks for making sure my apartment was clear and," she paused. "For helping with Bryan."

"He'll be back."

"Tell me something I don't know." She moved toward her front door.

"Is that why you started to text me today? Because of his visit last night?"

She paused with her hand on the door knob. "How did you know he was here last night?"

Suspicion flowed through her when he opened his mouth, closed it and then opened it again. "He said so."

She thought over what Bryan had said out the front of her building. At his unexpected appearance, surprise had held her in its clutches and anything he'd said after Carlos sprung out of the shadows hadn't penetrated her consciousness. "Okay, well, for tonight I'll be fine. I'll work out what I'm going to do tomorrow. Now, I'd like it if you left."

"Not happening, E. I'm staying." He crossed his arms over his impressive chest, the leather of his jacket tightening over his biceps. The man was too sexy and dangerous for his own good.

As much as she wanted to argue with him, her bed was calling and she was going to answer it. "I have a guest room, but that's for invited guests only, which you're not. Enjoy the couch."

Erin knew it was petty, but she didn't care. It was bad enough that she wouldn't be able to travel in the elevator without remembering how well he filled the space. The last thing she wanted was for him to insinuate himself into every room of her apartment. If she confined him to the living room then she could live with that.

"I've slept in worse places," he said, amusement lining every word.

Of course, he had.

"Night, Carlos."

"Night, Erin. Sweet dreams."

Erin walked out of the living room and down the hall to her bedroom, conscious of him watching her.

Sweet dreams? That would be hopeful. After visits from Bryan in the last two nights, and Carlos turning up as well, she had a feeling her dreams would be anything but sweet.

The buzzing of her alarm clock dissolved the dream she'd been having. Despite her expectations, she'd had dreams all right, although describing them as sweet would be wrong. More like hot and heavy, leaving her aching in a way she hadn't ached in years. All of her dreams included the man who was sleeping on her couch.

Exhaustion and unfulfilled lust tempted her to rollover to try and recapture the dream, a stupid desire. She and Carlos were over. Had been the moment he'd told her was going to enlist. The memory of him telling her still had the power to paralyze her. The fear that he may not return to her made their break up even harder. She'd hidden the hurt at the specter of him leaving during those last few weeks of school, had told him she was proud of him for wanting to protect and fight for his country. But part of her wanted to beg him to stay with her. Only she was moving to Colorado for college and if he stayed in New York, well, they probably wouldn't have lasted anyway. Better to have that clean break than a clingy one.

Over time, she'd pushed him so far down in her memories and deliberately stayed away from the people who could give her any information about him. Although she couldn't deny that whenever she heard on the news about military personnel who'd died overseas her heart leaped into her throat, and didn't return to the proper position until she knew for sure Carlos wasn't one of the ones killed.

A soft tap on the door drew her out of the dark space she'd fallen into. It opened slightly and an arm holding a coffee mug appeared.

"Coffee? You still take it with half a cup of milk so that it's more milk than java?"

He remembered how I like my coffee?

Her body still thrummed from repressed lust, so a bare chested Carlos walking in with her coffee conjured up images of him putting the mug on her bedside table, before he climbed on the bed and ravished her.

Her breathing quickened and she gripped the sheets to stop herself from running her fingers over his chest, tracing the outline of his impressive six pack, before settling at the waistband of his jeans. Once there she'd slip the button through the hole and slide the zipper down. Did he still wear boxer briefs or did he go commando now?

Mmmm commando.

"Erin? Are you okay?"

She waded through her lust to recall what he'd asked. "Oh yeah, coffee. Yes, I still have it milky and I'm fine. Just need my coffee to wake up."

"Honey, this," he held up the cup. "Is more warm milk than coffee. A cup of this isn't going to wake you up. It's going to put you to sleep."

Well, she wouldn't argue with the chance to have more sleep, especially if it was induced after a session of hot, sweaty, Carlos sex.

Whoa, girl. So not going to happen. He's not staying remember? He's going to leave you again at the drop of hat. Remember that.

Yes, the sensible voice was correct. She was going to ignore the fact the voice sounded like Antonia. Her best friend didn't belong in her bedroom—at all.

She sat up, the sheet falling away. She'd have to have been deaf not hear the sharp intake of Carlos's breath. She was wearing an old t-shirt, hardly a sexy lace negligée.

"Thanks for the coffee. You can leave now."

Please leave, otherwise I'm going to grab your arm and drag you to this bed and lick you all over.

"Uh-huh."

She glanced up at him and found his gaze wasn't on her face but on her chest. She wasn't huge, but she was pretty happy with her B cups. Her nipples tightened against the soft material and she was pretty sure a muffled groan came from Carlos's direction.

Her alarm buzzed again, breaking the sexual haze that threatened to pull them under.

"I have to get up," she said. "You know, work and all."

He hadn't moved from where he stood by the bed, but the moment he lifted his head and his gaze locked with hers, she wished she was looking somewhere else.

Desire licked out from his eyes, tempting her to do what she'd been thinking about the minute he walked into her room.

Her breath caught as he took a step closer. All he had to do was lean a knee on her mattress and she'd be dragging him down beside her.

"Erin," he whispered and then, as if working out where they were headed, he shook his head and took a step back. His clear rejection of following through on what had swirled around them should've annoyed her. Instead, she had to admit she was glad. Getting involved with him again was a bad idea.

A very bad idea.

C arlos strode out of Erin's room, his cock pressing hard against his zipper, demanding release. It would be a bad idea to get involved with Erin. But seeing her in her bed, the soft t-shirt hugging her in all the right places, memories of their past pummeled his brain.

They were each other's firsts. They'd fumbled through their first time together. After that he'd made sure he learned what gave her pleasure. He was a randy teenager, so anything got him off. But he wanted to make sure Erin had a good time, too.

As he entered her small kitchen, he grabbed another mug from the cupboard and poured his own coffee. He took a big gulp, enjoying the burn of the scalding liquid down his throat. What he needed to remember was that he wasn't here forever. He had one week to make sure she was safe before he had to report back to base in Virginia.

One week to ensure Bryan Tosconi was out of Erin's life for good.

For one week he could control his lust for Erin. But, fuck, it was going to be hard.

"Do you want anything to eat?"

He swiveled around to find Erin standing by the refrigerator, in nothing but the t-shirt she'd slept in.

Was she trying to kill him?

Oh yeah, he could think of something he'd like to eat, but it certainly wasn't food.

"What time do you need to leave?" he asked, even he could hear his voice was raspier than normal.

"Uh, I have to be out of here by 6:45."

He glanced at the green digital numbers on the microwave. "You going to be ready in half an hour? I don't believe it."

Her hands landed on her hips, cinching the t-shirt against her, pulling it higher up her legs. His body reacted and his dick hardened even more. He took a deep breath and tried to imagine anything but what Erin may or may not be wearing under that shirt. Did she sleep commando or did she have on some sexy, barely there, lace panties?

"You wanna bet?" she asked.

"Oh, honey, you don't wanna make a bet with me, you may not like my terms."

Flirting with Erin when she was wearing next to nothing was dangerous. But he liked to live dangerously. Hell he'd been living on danger's knife edge since he did the first job for the Forlani family.

"How about you listen to my terms?" she countered.

Carlos had a feeling he knew exactly where she was heading with her terms. "I'm listening."

"If I can get ready in thirty minutes, you'll stop *guarding* me."

Yep, exactly what he thought she'd say.

"Seeing as you're now down to twenty-five minutes the challenge is on. As for the other part of your terms, that's not negotiable. Last night should've shown you that you're not safe."

"Ugh, I knew you were going to say that. And Bryan is all bluster." A tell-tale blush crept up her neck. She never was very good at lying.

"Oh really, he's all bluster is he?"

"Yes." The blush deepened.

"Right. I suppose the week you took off last year where you didn't go anywhere or touch your bank accounts was because you wanted to take a week off work and chill and not see anyone."

Color leached out of her face. "What? How do you know that?"

"You're not denying it?"

"I uh." She ran her hand through her hair, her agitation and embarrassment reached out to him. He couldn't put her through this.

"Look, E, go get dressed. You don't want to be late for work."

Indecision flitted across her face. She looked like she wanted to argue further. Instead, she whirled around and walked out of the kitchen.

A breath whooshed out of Carlos. That wasn't how he wanted to let Erin know he knew about her situation. He should've kept it to himself. He wanted Erin to trust him. The chance of her trusting him now was pretty slim.

He had a lot of ground to make up. He only hoped she'd give him a chance to explain.

CHAPTER FIVE

The subway ride to work was not as unpleasant as she thought it was going to be with Carlos shadowing her. If someone got too close to her, either on the sidewalk or the train, he'd glare and they'd move away as if they'd been struck with an electric charge. She had to admit, it was nice to have a little breathing space on the packed commuter train.

A hand entered her vision and she looked up. Memories assailed her of the night she and Carlos had become an item. It had been at the homecoming dance of their junior year. She'd admired him for a year, ever since English class when he picked up her textbook and handed it to her. His brown eyes sparkled with mischief. She'd been lost and crushed on him so hard she was surprised the whole school hadn't teased her about it.

Even now her body shimmered with excitement at the sensation of when she put her hand in his. From that night until their Graduation Day, they'd been inseparable.

"It's our stop," he said as he leaned close to her so she could hear him.

"Okay." And just like she did all those years ago, she placed her hand in his and he pulled her up until her body was aligned with his. The train jerked to a halt, pitching their bodies forward. He tightened his arm around her to prevent her from falling. Her breath caught in her throat and it took everything in her not to lean up and bury her nose into his neck.

The doors opened and people clamored to get off. With his arm still anchoring her to his side, Carlos guided them out to the platform.

Knowing she needed to get herself back under control, and her mind on the present and not the past, Erin extracted herself from his grip once they were out of the station. "I'll be okay now. The hotel is a couple of blocks away."

"Fine. Lead on."

"Seriously, Carlos, you don't need to babysit me. I've survived in this big bad city by myself for the last ten years."

"That was before you met Bryan."

Exasperation filled her and she slapped his hand away when he went to cup her elbow. "Look, you can take your arrogant Navy SEALness and go take a hike. Isn't that what you guys do? Push your body until you're all hot and sweaty and feeling like you conquered the world?"

The corner of his mouth lifted into a sexy grin. "Honey, I can think of a far better way to get hot, sweaty, and feeling like I conquered the world. And trust me when I say, it doesn't involve hiking anywhere."

"You are impossible," she muttered and turned away from him. If she didn't, she'd throw her arms around his neck and tell him she was on board for hot and sweaty.

Fuck, she needed her head read. Hadn't she already determined that taking a walk down memory lane with Carlos was the worst thing she could do.

With her shoulders back and her focus on getting to work on time, she started down the sidewalk. It was becoming clearer and clearer that no matter how much she wanted him to go away and leave her alone, Carlos would be trailing her every move. Didn't he have anything better to do than to follow her to and from work? What was he planning to do, sit and guard her office? No way, that wasn't happening.

She marched through the revolving door and nodded to the concierge and the two staff members manning the check-in desk. Her only goal was to reach her office. If the staff thought it funny that a guy was following her, they knew better than to say anything. Although she was pretty sure gossip would be flying around the hotel that a hunky man had disappeared into the executive offices with her.

Once she was standing behind her desk, she deigned to talk to him. "Right, well I'm here. Safe and sound. I don't plan on leaving my office today. So, thank you for your escort, but your services are no longer needed." She waved her hand in the air. "Run along now. Do whatever you SEALS do."

Erin turned away from him and shrugged out of her coat. She hung it on the coat rack, taking way longer than necessary. She still hadn't heard the door open or close signaling Carlos had left.

God, she needed a coffee. After their *chat* in the kitchen she hadn't been able to drink it. Maybe everything wouldn't be so annoying or stressful once she'd drunk that first cup of java. Bracing herself to see Carlos leaning sexily against the doorframe, she faced her office door, only to find it shut and Carlos nowhere to be seen.

Damn, those sneaky SEAL skills.

C arlos gazed out the window, watching the entrance to Erin's hotel as he sipped his glass of water. He was hoping the liquid would cool his jets. They'd been firing on all cylinders since he'd walked into Erin's bedroom. Seeing her all rumpled, with sexy bed hair, had his body standing to attention.

His phone vibrated on the table. A quick look had a smile breaking out over his face.

"Ma! How's Florida."

"Hot and humid, but wonderful. Dad's on his boat, again."

Carlos smiled at the joy in mom's voice. He was glad his folks were happy. They'd struggled through life, dad working down on the docks, while mom looked after him and his brother. Fortune struck them two years ago when they'd won the lottery. Now they'd retired to Florida and were enjoying their new-found riches. They'd offered him some money, but he'd turned them down. He enjoyed his job, even though it was danger-ous. He didn't need their money to make him happy. His brother, on the other hand, had taken the money and the last Carlos knew, David, was living it up in Monte Carlo. If he knew his brother, David would soon be heading back to the US having blown through the money. But he would've had a great time.

"So what can I do for ya, Ma?"

"Nothing, I wanted to say hello. I don't get to do that often while you're away."

He closed his eyes at the concern replacing her joyful tone. He hated that his job choice distressed her so much, but he couldn't be anything other than a SEAL. The moment he started training, he knew he'd found where he belonged. "I love you, Ma."

"I love you, too. I'm very proud of you, even though you worry me so much."

"I've always worried you," he chuckled, hoping to lighten the mood between them.

"That you do. So where are you? Are you in Virginia?"

"Nah, I'm in New York."

"New York? Why? You never visited us when we still lived there?"

There was censure in her tone and he knew he deserved it. How could he tell his mom he hadn't wanted to go back to see her in case he saw some of his old crew? He'd kept his work with the mob hidden from her. He had no doubt Dad suspected his oldest son was involved in some shady business. Dad never said anything to him though and Carlos supposed it was because Dad was protecting Mom as much as he was.

Plus, he hadn't wanted to give into the temptation to look Erin up and see how she was going. Hell, he'd lasted sixteen years without seeing her. One phone call from Ash and he'd done whatever needed to be done to help his friend. What kind of son did that make him? He wouldn't go see Mom and Dad, meaning if they wanted to see him they had to make the effort.

He really was an asshole.

"I know, Ma. I had my reasons."

"It's okay I understand. I do. You did what you had to do. I'm proud of you."

He heard a buzzing sound. "What's that?"

"Oh, that's my cookies. I gotta go. Good chat. I love you."

"Bye, Ma. Love you too."

He placed his phone back on the table, memories of Mom's chocolate chip cookies filling his mind. It had been a long time since he'd had some. He should ask her for a care package.

The door to the café opened and he looked up, his

gaze connecting with a venomous one. His back straightened and he matched Bryan's glare. He'd stared down plenty of shady characters on the job, he could handle this wanna-be mobster.

Bryan strode over to his table. Even from a distance Carlos could see the intent in his body language. The douche was spoiling for a fight.

Shit, the last thing he needed was to get into an altercation with him, but if that's what the fucker wanted, he would give him one. Carlos didn't need an automatic weapon in his hand to be dangerous.

If the man was here in front of him, at least that meant Erin was safe in her office. When Carlos arrived at the café he'd fired off a message to Tex to see if he could get some information on Bryan. He was still waiting to hear back. If he wanted to, he could probably find out everything about Bryan himself.

Bryan sat down opposite him. "Who the fuck are you to Erin? I don't believe you when you say you're her boyfriend."

Carlos leaned back and folded his arms over his chest. "I'm a person you don't want to mess with, sunshine."

"You don't scare me. And you still haven't answered my question."

It took everything in Carlos not to reach over the table and grab the jerk by the throat. If he didn't want to find himself in deep shit with his team and Commander, he need to control the urge. The guy wasn't worth it. But the jerk needed to be warned away from Erin.

"I don't have to answer your questions. What I am to Erin is none of your damn business." He stood and leaned over the table so he was looking down on Bryan. "Just know this. You come anywhere near her and you will live to regret it."

CHAPTER SIX

"Geez, Carlos, I don't need you to follow me *everywhere*." All she wanted was some space. Some time alone, which was friggin' impossible with Carlos shadowing her every move. Well, she couldn't deny with him accompanying her to and from work every day it had guaranteed her a seat on the subway. One look from Carlos and the person sitting would get up and offer her their seat.

That was the only advantage of him following her. The girls at the front desk all swooned when he walked in. She couldn't blame them. The man knew how to wear a black t-shirt and faded jeans.

"I still don't trust Bryan. He's been too quiet."

"And that's a bad thing? Maybe he got picked up by the cops again?" It seemed an unlikely scenario, but she could hope.

"No. He hasn't. He's still lurking around."

Erin didn't bother to hide the roll of her eyes. "And you know this, how?"

He leaned back against her kitchen counter, one leg crossed over the other. If someone didn't know him they'd think he was relaxed. After living with him for the last three days, Erin knew Carlos didn't relax. In fact, she wasn't sure he'd even slept. He was awake when she went to bed and awake when her alarm went off.

"Trust me. I know."

She canted her head to the side, studying him closely. "What aren't you telling me?"

"The less you know the better."

His casual dismissal was the last straw. "Oh no you don't. You don't get to stand in my kitchen and treat me like I'm an annoying bug. I'm a grown woman."

Her words had Carlos standing up a little straighter. His gaze traveled down her body, lingering at her breasts. Her nipples hardened, pushing against the lace of her bra.

"Believe me when I say I *know* you're a grown woman."

The vibe in the room changed. Gone was the casual atmosphere. Sexual attraction sizzled and arced through the air. If she closed her eyes right now, she knew she'd be seeing his tattooed bare chest. Ever since that first morning when he'd walked into her room, she'd been wanting to see his chest again. To trace her tongue around the tattoos that hadn't been there when they'd first dated.

Did each one have a story? Her tongue slipped out to moisten her dry lips. His groan vibrated around the room.

In two strides he was by her side. His hands slid up her arms until they framed her face. Her resolve to not get close to him melted. They'd been dancing around each other since he'd shown back up in her life. Resisting his touch was a useless endeavor. It always had been.

"Erin," he whispered as he lowered his head toward her. Her heart rate kicked up a notch. How did he manage to get so much emotion simply by saying her name?

Rational thought left her the minute his lips touched hers. She clutched his t-shirt so she didn't collapse in a heap at his feet.

Magical.

That was the only way she could describe being back in Carlos's arms. She moaned against his lips and opened her mouth wider, allowing his tongue to slip in. His hands moved from her face and wrapped around her shoulders bringing her closer to him. Heat pooled between her legs and she wanted nothing more than to take this from her kitchen to her bedroom.

It had been so long since someone made her feel special. Bryan had never taken the time to kiss her like this. Like if this was all he could have, then it would be enough for him. Kissing Carlos had always been like that. Back in high school, even though he'd been rough around the edges, when he was with her he'd been nothing but a gentleman. It had been she who'd encouraged him to round the bases.

He pulled away from her, breaking their connection.

"What? Why?" The words tumbled out.

"My phone's ringing."

Irritation replaced the haze of desire clouding her. His phone was more important than her?

"By all means, answer the phone. Far be it from me to stop you." Okay, so she sounded way more bitter than she should be.

"Honey, I can't ignore my phone. It could be my Commander."

Shame at her selfishness hit her. Over the past three days she'd put his dangerous job to the back of her mind. If she didn't think about it then it couldn't hurt her.

"Sorry," she mumbled.

He nodded and strode over to where he'd left his phone. "Damn," he muttered when the call ended as he picked it up.

"Was it your Commander?" She shoved her hands into the back pocket of her jeans in an attempt to stop herself from reaching out and touching him again.

"No."

"Right, well I think I might—uh—I think I'll take a shower."

"Okay."

Great, they were down to one syllable replies. Who the heck had called him? If it wasn't his Commander, then wouldn't he be relieved? Maybe he wanted to get called away from her.

No.

She squashed the thought. If he was so anxious to get away from her, he wouldn't have kissed her senseless not two minutes ago.

Erin had almost reached her bedroom door, when he called her name. She turned to face him.

"Do you want to go out tonight?"

An invitation to go out was the last thing she expected to come out of his mouth. "Pardon? I don't think I heard that correctly."

His lips quirked into a sinfully sexy smile. Damn, that needed to come with a warning. "You heard me fine. Can you be done in half an hour?"

Erin was convinced her hallway had become a portal to an alternate universe, because not thirty seconds ago, Carlos was responding to her with one syllable answers. Whatever had switched in him, she was going to grab it with both hands and run with it. A night out sounded like a great idea.

"Yeah I can be."

"Great, and bring a jacket."

With that last instruction, he turned and disappeared into the room he'd claimed as his own while he stayed with her.

She shook her head and walked into her bedroom, the man's mood swings were worse than a woman's during PMS.

E rin licked her ice cream as she walked through Central Park. Carlos walked beside her licking his own cone. Who knew eating ice cream could be so sexy? The way his tongue curled around the frozen treat fired up the desire that had been simmering beneath the surface all night.

"Is spring still your favorite season?" he asked her.

Her step faltered. He remembered her favorite season. Who was this man? From chatter with her girl-friends, most guys didn't remember what their girl-friends had worn the day before, let alone remember something from over sixteen years ago.

"Yes."

"When you're away as much as I am, you don't notice the change in seasons. One minute you're knee deep in snow in South America. The next the sun is beating down on your back in some god-forsaken desert."

A door opened a crack, giving her an insight into the person Carlos had become, the life he'd led over the last decade and half. A life she'd not been privileged to share with him. Could she be a military wife, never knowing if her man was going to come back to her alive and whole?

She liked to think she could do it, but she hadn't been given the opportunity to find out. Well, no, that wasn't quite right. Even though they hadn't said the words to each other, they both knew after graduation they would be going their separate ways.

"Is it hard?" she asked, as she grabbed his hand and pulled him toward a park bench. If they were going to have a conversation like this, they were going to do it sitting down facing each other.

"Yes. It can be the hardest, shittiest job in the world some days. Other days it's the most rewarding job ever."

She soaked up his words and let them simmer inside her a little longer. She'd seen the movies depicting SEAL teams. Had always wondered if they portrayed everything real teams went through. Somehow Erin knew reality was completely different to Hollywood.

"How long are you usually away for?"

He shrugged. "Depends. Some missions are short. Some are long. If it's a long mission it's better not to think about the amount of days going past. Each one kind of blends into the other."

"Do you have any contact with anyone from home while you're away?"

"Not usually. We can't and don't talk about missions."

"Do you mean that your family can't know where you are? Or if you're in a relationship your partner has no idea as well?" That shocked the heck out of her. How on earth did the families cope with that?

"It's not ideal, but it's what we do. Plus the guys on my team are all single. Relationships don't work too well when you can't be forthcoming with what your job entails."

"I can imagine," she murmured. Could she do it? Could she give herself over to Carlos, knowing that when he left she'd have no idea where he was going?

Whoa. She needed to slow down this runaway horse. He'd been back in her life for three days. Well, okay, a bit longer than that seeing as it was a couple of months ago he came around asking for information about some of the guys he'd hung out with as a teenager. He'd walked into a coffee shop in Little Italy and she'd almost dropped her drink in her lap. It had been the first time in months that she'd gone to the area she'd grown up in. And of all the days she did, Carlos walked in.

Now here they were, eating ice cream in Central Park after having hot dogs from a cart. It turned out to be a perfect night. One she wouldn't forget. Carlos was opening up to her. Sharing parts of his life she hadn't known about, but had spent the last sixteen years wondering about.

"Why hotel management?"

The question pulled her from her thoughts. "Pardon?"

"Why did you go into hotel management? I thought you wanted to go into accounting. Wasn't that what you told me?"

How the heck did he remember a long ago conversation they'd shared laying on the roof of the apartment building where he'd lived, their fingers touching. She'd been so young and naïve thinking that all his talk of joining the military after graduation had been just that— talk. Until the day he'd shown her the brochures he'd

70

gotten at the recruiters. She'd known then that not even her telling him she loved him would keep him by her side.

"Accounting wasn't quite where I wanted to spend the rest of my life. Hotel management gives me the chance to see the world. I found I liked interacting with people, too."

"And have you seen the world?"

"Yep, I spent three years in France, traveled all over Europe. Best time of my life."

They sat in silence, lost in their own thoughts, as they finished their ice cream. Night had closed in on them as they'd been strolling through the park. She should feel frightened. No way in hell would she wander around the park in the dark by herself. With Carlos by her side, she felt safe, like she'd always felt when he had been by her side. It would be nice to feel like this forever.

A sigh gusted out of her and his arm landed around her shoulder, as though he could read her mind.

"We should head back," he said.

I don't want to. She bit the words back. If they went back, she was worried that Bryan would be waiting for her. It didn't matter that she hadn't seen or heard from him in the last three days. He was still lurking around. She knew he was. Waiting for the moment when he could strike when she least expected it.

It had been comforting to have Carlos by her side as she'd walked up to her building. But she knew he couldn't be in New York forever. He had a job and a duty to his country. No matter how much she was beginning to wish his duty was to her only. A dangerous thought and one she needed to crush before it could take hold.

"When do you leave?" she asked, even though she didn't want to know.

"I have to be back at base in two days."

"Where's your base? On the West Coast?"

His finger picked up a stray tendril of her hair, the tension tightening within her with every twirl of his finger.

"Virginia."

"Oh, I didn't know they had a base there. I thought it was all on the west coast, you know in San Diego."

"Yes."

Okay, we're back to one syllable answers. Parts of their earlier conversation came back to her. Did not talking about his missions include not talking about where his base was? No, she didn't think it was that important to keep quiet. Or was he not saying anything because he didn't want her surprising him with a visit. Not that she'd ever do that. He may turn up uninvited, but she wouldn't, no matter how much she may need or want to see him.

A clean break again between them would be the best thing to do.

"You're right. It's time to leave."

CHAPTER SEVEN

The trip back to Erin's place had been more torturous than some of the things he'd had to endure during BUD/S training. Her attitude toward him had changed after she asked him where he was based.

He could've told her the exact name of the base, but he didn't want to. He was worried if he did, he'd tell her to come visit him. And that was the worst thing he could do. Nothing good would come with picking up where they'd left off all those years ago. No matter how much he wanted to. No matter how much his *body* wanted to. When he'd made his first SEAL team he'd made the decision to make his career his life. Families and SEAL life didn't always mesh. He needed to remember that.

As they walked up the steps to her apartment he scanned the area. Tex had been keeping an eye on Bryan and if he got anywhere near Erin's place he'd phone Carlos. So far, his phone had remained silent, but that didn't mean he slacked off from his duty. The itching in his palm had settled down. He wasn't stupid enough to think that his warning a few days ago in the coffee shop was enough for the other man to stay away permanently. If he knew anything about mob life, and he knew a bit from experience, Bryan was probably laying low until Carlos left town before he struck again.

There in lay his problem. What did he do? He knew his commitment, first and foremost, was to his team. No questions asked. He wouldn't let his team down. On the other hand, he didn't want to leave Erin vulnerable.

Fuck, he'd known venturing down the path of his old life would lead to complications. He just hadn't expected the complications to lead to the woman standing in front of him. He'd figured it would be Rico who would give him a hard time about leaving the neighborhood and the gang. Figured they'd do what they could to drag him back in. He was a lot stronger now than he'd been back then, when the need to help out his parents clouded his sensibilities.

"Are you planning on standing out there all night?" Erin interrupted his thoughts. "Because I don't have a problem with you doing that."

Pulling on the mental toughness that had seen him through many hell-in-a-hand-basket ops, he climbed the final two steps and met her on the stoop. Her sweet, flowery perfume tugged at his senses.

God, how he wanted to lose himself in her one more time. As callous as it sounded, one final goodbye before he went back to base. A beautiful memory he could pull out when things got too hard to bear while overseas.

Acting purely on need and adrenaline, he grabbed Erin's hand and pulled her into the foyer of her building, his senses ignoring the pungent smell of the potpourri. He had one goal in mind. That was him, Erin and bed, and fuck the consequences.

The elevator doors opened and he propelled her inside.

"Carlos? What the fuck is go—" He swallowed the rest of her words as his lips crashed down on hers.

He groaned as a cloud of peace settled over him. Yes, this was right. This was perfect. This could be one night only.

Carlos knew the moment the fight went out of her. Her body melted against his. Her arms wrapped around his neck and her mouth opened wider, giving him the access he needed.

The bell signaling they'd reached the floor, registered in his sub-consciousness. Maintaining his hold on her he guided them out of the lift and to her front door. He broke the kiss long enough to reach into his pocket to extract the key she'd given him. His hand shook as he inserted the key and unlocked the door.

The second she slammed it shut behind them, his mouth was on Erin's. He scooped her up in his arms and carried her down the hall to her bedroom.

Ever since that first day when he'd walked into the white and blue room, he'd wanted nothing more than to be in her bed. Now he was going to get that wish and he was going to make it a night she would never forget.

Because he knew he never would.

Over the past sixteen years he'd buried their past and his feelings for her, excused them as teenage infatuation that would never last into adulthood. How wrong he'd been. The old saying absence makes the heart grow stronger floated through his mind. Every fucking word was true. Without him knowing, his feelings for Erin hadn't died, they'd grown. Expanded into an all encompassing need he could no longer deny.

He still loved Erin. She was his one and only. And while they had this night, he would walk away from her. Because walking away was the best for the both of them. He couldn't put her through the pain of never knowing if he was coming home to her. He'd distanced himself from his family for this very reason. It hurt, but it was for the best. He was going to make the most of tonight.

When he reached the side of her bed, he lowered her legs so she was standing. He kept an arm firmly around her, not wanting to let her go for even a second.

"What's happening here, Carlos?" she whispered, her breathing ragged. With her hair mussed and her lips plump and shiny from his kisses, words seemed impossible to form. Words needed to be said.

Honest words.

"It's simple, honey. I'm going to do what I've been wanting to do since I saw you when I walked into *Papa's* café three months ago." He reached out and traced a finger down her cheek. "I need you, E. Need you so much."

Carlos held his breath, waiting to see if she was going to throw him out of her bedroom. The way she kissed him back, he didn't think kicking him out was the upper most thought of her mind. At least he hoped it wasn't.

A slow, sexy smile formed on her face. An answering one pulled at his lips. Yeah, there was no way she was throwing him out.

Erin's hand landed flat on his chest, and blood rushed to his second head. He'd never gotten so hard, so quickly by a woman putting her hands on his chest. "This could be a really bad mistake," she husked out.

"You're not telling me something I haven't already told myself. But sometimes mistakes turn out to be the best thing to ever happen to you."

As her fingers tiptoed up his chest, he struggled to not capture them in his hands and hold them behind her back so he could ravish her. Instead, he let her have free reign. It had been so long since she'd touched him. As part of his need to memorize every detail of their encounter, he didn't want to stop her from doing anything she wanted to him.

"You're leaving in a couple of days." Her hands smoothed over his shoulder and looped around his neck.

"I know." He leaned forward and nipped her earlobe. As much as he wanted to possess her, he wouldn't do it if she didn't want him to. Antonia's words from the other night sounded in his head.

You've already hurt her once.

Was giving into his primal needs a selfish move? He had to ask.

Reaching up he unhooked her hands from around his neck and held them in front of him. "Do you want me to stop? I will. Just say the word. I can't promise you anything more than tonight."

"I know and if you even think about stopping, I won't be held responsible for what I do." Her fingers crushed his shirt, and her lips landed on his.

There was his answer. No mistaking what she wanted. It matched what he wanted. The guilt at only giving her one night flew out the window. If she wanted him to stop, he would've done it. Even though it would've been the hardest thing he'd ever had to do, walk away from her. He would've done it. She meant that much to him.

Her mouth roved over his, her teeth nipping at his bottom lip. He granted her access. But it wasn't enough. He wanted more. He wanted the feel of her flesh beneath his fingers. Her body naked and writhing beneath his. He wanted to get lost in burying himself balls deep into her tight, warm, sheath. He wanted it all.

It seemed she was as frantic as he was. Their hands attacked their clothing. Pulling at fabric so they could be skin to skin, breaking their kiss long enough to get rid of tops before connecting again.

Carlos wanted to slow things down so he could fulfill his plan of storing their night in his memory banks. Erin didn't seem to want slow. Slow was overrated.

He almost lost his load when her fingers brushed his aching cock to pull his zipper down. No, he needed to slow things down. He reached down and removed her hand. Sparks fired through him when she bit his lip in protest.

He chuckled. "We've got all night. We don't need to rush."

"Ugh, you don't know how long it's been since I had a decent orgasm."

Carlos liked a challenge and if that douche Bryan hadn't had the balls to make sure Erin's needs were taken care of, he had no such qualms. "Well then, I better make sure it's one you never forget."

Now he definitely need to make sure he took it slow. With sure movements he dispensed with her jeans so she stood before him in her underwear. Damn, she looked even more beautiful than he recalled. The first time they'd slept together they were both still teenagers. Erin hadn't grown into her curves. She had now and he couldn't wait to explore them.

"Do you have any idea how good it is to look at you?" he asked.

"Almost as good as seeing you. But I think you've got more clothes on than me."

Man he liked her sassy mouth. "Well then, I think I can remedy that."

His hands went to the waistband of his jeans, but she stopped him from undoing the button.

"No you don't. You removed mine, I think it's only fair that I remove yours."

Her eyes sparkled with mischief. He'd do anything to keep that look in her eyes. Somehow Carlos didn't think Erin was going to be as swift as him. He held his hands up in mock surrender. "I'm all yours, honey."

The muscles in his stomach quivered when she rubbed her fingertips along the inside of his jeans. Yep, she planned to take her time. If he wasn't careful he could really embarrass himself. Erin had said it had been a while since she'd had an orgasm. It had been a while since *he'd* slept with someone.

Finally, her hand wandered back to his button, undid it and then lowered his zipper. He helped her remove his jeans until he stood in front of her in his boxer briefs. Her fingers reached out and traced his tattoos.

"They're beautiful," she whispered. "I don't normally like tattoos, but these only enhance who you are. Do they mean anything?"

The last thing he wanted to talk about was his tatts. He had way more important things he wanted to do.

"Not really what I want to talk about, E." To prove his point, he wrapped her up in his arms and lowered his head towards her. "Talking is overrated, didn't you know that?"

He sipped at her lips before trailing down her neck. His hands roamed up her back, pausing when he reached her bra clip. With a quick flick, the fabric separated and he pulled the straps down her arm, freeing her breasts. Her back arched as he brushed a thumb across her nipple. His cock strained against the cotton of his boxers. It would be so easy to rip them and her panties down, bury himself so deeply in her they wouldn't know where each other started or ended.

"Why are you taking so long?" she asked, thrusting her hips against his groin, her message for what she wanted to happen as clear as clean glass.

"I'm not a wham bam thank you ma'am type of guy."

Her fingernails clawed into his back. He didn't mind the bite of pain shooting through him. "I wish you were."

"Maybe later. This time, I'm taking it slow."

"Slow is overrated."

He chuckled at her saying the words he'd thought about earlier and tweaked her nipple. "Slow is the best type, honey."

Carlos captured her lips again, as his fingers massaged her breasts, his heart pounding in his ears. With his lips still connected to hers, he maneuvered them until they lay on her bed, the mattress soft beneath their bodies.

Her hands floated down his back until they reached his ass. He tensed his glutes, expecting the sting of her nails through the thin material. Instead she squeezed and it was all he could do not to give into the wham bam thank you ma'am scenario she wanted.

Reaching down, he found the edge of her panties. He hooked a finger around the thin elastic and tugged it down. Her legs lifted to help him remove her last item of clothing. The scent of her arousal wafted up and he shimmered down her body. Leaning in, he placed a gentle kiss on the top of her pubic bone, before running a tongue up her slick folds.

A moan escaped out of her. She tasted so good. He flicked at the small bundle of nerves and slipped a finger inside of her.

"Fuck, Carlos, that feels so good."

He smiled against her neck, looked like his Erin's mouth got dirty now while having sex. It would be a lie to say he didn't like it. He did, a lot. With sure strokes of his tongue and finger, he brought her to her first climax. The sound of her crying out his name was music to his ears. The time of going slow was over.

Kissing his way up her body, he brought her down from the high of her orgasm. It wouldn't be long before she was back there again. Once he reached her lips he possessed them in a soft kiss. Her hands returned to his briefs and she tugged on them, he added his own hands and together they removed them.

"Condoms?" he asked, pleased he still had a smattering of sensibility to make sure Erin was protected. An image of her body swelling with a child blasted through him. An impossible dream. A dream he'd never allowed himself to have. A dream he was finding he wanted to fulfill.

"Top drawer." The sultry tone of her voice doing nothing to dissipate the dream of a life with her that was beginning to blossom in his mind.

No. You only have tonight. Don't forget it. Don't

forget your job. It's not conducive to a lasting relationship that included kids.

How he wanted to throat punch that voice, no matter how right it was. And why the fuck was he letting these thoughts take over his mind? He was minutes away from burying himself deep into Erin's pussy.

He'd promised himself he would give her mind-blowing orgasms, and he would. She'd had one. He still had plenty in him to give her at least two more.

With his head back in the game, he reached across and pulled open the top drawer of her bedside table. Scrambling around the contents his fingers closed over a square box. He rolled over and opened the box, pulling out a strip of rubbers. He ripped one off and placed the others, along with the box, back on the top of the table.

"Let me," Erin purred as she grabbed the condom from his fingers.

Carlos smiled and laid back. "Be my guest."

When her hand ran down the length of his body and grabbed his rock hard dick, he wondered if it had been a smart decision to let her take control. It had been a while since he'd buried himself balls deep in a woman he cared about. In fact, he would hazard a guess it was sixteen years ago. Every encounter, and there hadn't been a lot of them, had been more about slaking a need, than anything emotional.

A feather-light touch on the head of his cock had his eyes closing and his fists clenching the sheets. To stop himself from blowing his load in her hand, he directed his thoughts to the place he went to when doing his grueling PT every morning. He bit back a groan when she rolled the thin latex over his flesh.

The moment she took her fingers away, he wrapped an arm around her waist and flipped her over so that he was lying on top of her again.

Once he'd nestled himself at her entrance he hooked a finger under her chin and lifted her head so their gazes met. He wanted to be looking at her when he joined their bodies.

"Ready?" he asked.

"Yes."

Before he pushed into her, he reached down and stroked her a couple of times. Her hips lifted instinctively, telling him she was more than ready for the next step. He adjusted the angle of his hips and guided himself into her body. Her warmth enclosed him and he couldn't stop the groan of pleasure eking out of him.

"God, this feels so good," he said when he was buried deep inside her.

"You have no idea how unbelievable this feels," she breathed.

With their gazes still connected, he began to move slowly. Retreating and advancing in measured strokes. Erin's hips met his every push forward and followed when he pulled out.

"Faster, Carlos."

"Yes." He wanted that as much as she did. Raising himself on his elbows he increased his pace. Her inner muscles clenched him tightly before releasing him for a fraction of a second, then gripping him again. The sensation wasn't like anything he'd ever experienced before. He could feel his balls tingling. His climax was imminent and he wanted Erin to join him when he went over the edge. Adding a hand to where they were joined, he massaged her tight bud. Her short breaths indicated she was close—again. Erin's body shuddered around him as another orgasm washed over her. He kept thrusting through the trembles of her body, until she cried out again and this time he joined her over the edge. His release pounding through him and into her. He slowed his movements until little quakes hit them both every now and then.

Exhausted, he rolled over, taking her with him. Tucking her against his side, he kissed her sweaty forehead.

Carlos acknowledged the sense of peace that filtered through him. A sensation he hadn't felt in a long time. He knew it was all due to the person lying in his arms. "Thank you," he whispered, before he welcomed sleep's embrace.

CHAPTER EIGHT

Feather light kisses trailed down her spine as a hand crept up to cup her breast. If this was how she was going to be woken up every morning, there'd be no argument coming from her. It sure as hell beat the buzzing of an alarm clock.

"I could get used to this," she stretched and mumbled at the same time. The hand caressing her breast stop and the long male body behind her froze.

Shit, probably not what he wanted to hear.

She rolled over and faced him. "Hey, I know it's not going to happen, but I'm going to enjoy this morning's wake up call, okay?"

Indecision had his eyes narrowing, as though he wanted to believe her but wasn't sure he actually did. Erin wanted to make the most of the morning. A feeling began to grow inside her that when she walked out of the hotel today, Carlos wouldn't be standing to the side, waiting for her, regardless of the fact he'd told her he wasn't needed back at base for a couple days. It hadn't taken long for her to get used to having him close by, even though she'd initially hated the idea.

Taking matters into her own hands she reached down and stroked his hard cock, which was resting against her thigh.

"One last time," she whispered against his lips. "Make it one to remember."

She didn't care if she sounded desperate, as she kissed him, her hands increasing their motion along his hard length. With each upward motion, the tension seemed to ease out of him. She knew she'd won him over when he gripped her hand and covered her body with his.

Never would she ever forget the feeling of the weight of his body lying against hers. Whenever she and Bryan had slept together, which wasn't as often as he wanted but was plenty enough for her, all she'd wanted to do was push him off her. She'd never suffered from claustrophobia when she'd slept with a guy. Bryan was the exception to the rule.

Thoughts of Bryan and their disastrous sex life disappeared from her mind the second Carlos entered her body. When they'd been exploring their sex life as teenagers, they'd fumbled around each other the first couple of times. It had been amazing for her, then, but it was out of the world amazing now.

She closed her eyes and gave herself over to the bliss her body was feeling as Carlos worked himself in and out of her. Her legs wrapped around his waist, gripping him tighter as her orgasm spiraled through her.

Yeah her vibrator wasn't going to give her the same release as being with Carlos did.

The sound of their ragged breathing echoed around her bedroom as they came down from the heights. Her limbs were so loose, standing and walking to the shower seemed impossible.

For the first time in her life she wished she didn't have to go to work. Unfortunately, her position didn't allow her the luxury of calling in sick.

"I need to move," she said.

"Yeah, I suppose you do." Carlos responded, but he tightened his grip on her. Did he not want to let her go? Was it as hard for him to let go as it was for her to pull away?

One last kiss and then she'd get out of bed.

One kiss led to Carlos following her into the shower, which led to some amazing shower sex. Now here they were walking toward her hotel. Their fingers entwined and with each step they took, their paced slowed.

When they reached the art deco building Carlos tugged her toward him. She rested her hands against his hard chest. She'd run her tongue over every little rise and fall of his six pack.

"Will I see you tonight?" she asked, cringing at the pleading tone she tried hard to hide.

"Yeah. My flight is first thing tomorrow morning."

"Dinner out somewhere?"

He shrugged as if he didn't care, but she knew

differently. They have may have spent a decade and half apart, but some things didn't change. When Carlos was acting like he didn't care, it meant he cared an awful lot.

"I'll take that as a yes. I'll see you at six." She leaned up on her tiptoe and kissed him on the lips. Even though the temptation to linger was strong, she didn't give into it.

She swiveled on her heel and strode into the hotel, smiling at the staff, even though inside she was trying very hard not to let the tears fall.

Tomorrow morning was going to be a bitch.

Carlos watched the door of the hotel slide shut, closing off his view of Erin. He blew out a breath and rolled his shoulders in an attempt to release some of his tension. Sadly, he was beginning to believe the tension was going to be a bed partner for a long while. Not the type of bed partner he wanted, but it was one he would have to put up with.

Eventually the longing and need for Erin would fade away, like it had done when he'd first walked away from her.

And ISIS will stop bombing innocents.

He shook his head and crossed the road to sit at the café so he could watch Erin's building.

"Hey there, Carlos. You want your usual?" Mac, the young barista behind the counter called out to him. The guy was the epitome of a millennial, long hair pulled back into a messy man-bun, scruff outlining his chin. Every time he looked at the guy, Carlos's hand went to his own beard. His was neater than Mac's, and nowhere near as long.

"Thanks, that would be great. I'll have a ham and cheese breakfast sandwich, too."

Because he'd joined Erin in the shower, he hadn't had time to get something to eat. As he sat, he let his mind wander to the previous evening and morning. He wouldn't change any second of it, even knowing that come tomorrow, he'd be walking away from her—again.

"Here you go." Mac placed his drink and sandwich on the table.

"Thanks." Carlos expected the other man to walk away, but he hovered by the table. "You need something else, Mac?"

"Look, I don't know if this will make sense to you, but..."

Carlos's left palm started itching. "I'm sure it will."

Mac's shoulders relaxed at his words. "Well, there was this guy in here asking about you, which I found weird, because prior to this week you've never shown up here before. Anyway, he asked if you still came in."

"What did you tell him?"

"I said yes. He left after that. But anyway, I thought I'd mention it."

Carlos held out his hand and Mac shook it. "Thanks, man."

"Anytime."

Mac went back to his position behind the counter and Carlos picked up his coffee, inhaling deeply and letting the fragrant scent consume him.

He hadn't exactly been covert in his movements, and he knew Bryan had seen him in here on occasion. The fact he was asking if Carlos still came in was a clear indication that Bryan was biding his time, waiting until Carlos was gone enabling Bryan to make his move on Erin.

Fuck.

This was the last thing he needed with his flight out tomorrow. How the hell was he going to keep Erin safe if he wasn't watching her? Oh, he knew he couldn't continually watch her. He had a job to do, a team who relied on him. He wasn't going to let them down.

Giving Erin's building another look, he was relieved to see that nobody appeared to be loitering around the entrance. Could he talk to the doorman, show him a picture of Bryan and tell the guy not to let the scumbag in?

He was pretty sure the staff of the hotel loved Erin and would do anything for her. He'd seen how they all treated her on the odd occasion he'd walked her to her office. But to ask the favor would be letting the staff in on Erin's private life. A fact he knew she wouldn't appreciate.

Maybe Tex could help him out. Although it was a lot to ask of the guy. Carlos knew Tex did a lot of stuff for the military, which included watching a couple of teams. Or maybe he could get Ash to help out. Maybe he had a former PI contact who could watch Erin.

But even getting her protected was really only a band-aid solution. The only sure way to keep Erin safe was if Bryan was put behind bars again. This time without the possibility of his gang of lawyers bailing him out again.

He reached into his pocket, pulled out his phone, and hit Tex's number. The phone went to voicemail. "Hey Tex, it's Italy. I need to speak to you about my situation. Call me when you get a chance."

Next, he called, Ash, his former teammate.

"Riley Ashland."

"Ash, Italy here."

"Italy, how are you? How much longer are you in the big apple?"

Carlos had felt bad about upping and leaving Ash's place after not even spending one night there. He shouldn't have worried. His former teammate had had no issues with Carlos staying at Erin's place once he knew she was being harassed by Bryan. "I fly out tomorrow morning at seven."

"Nice and early."

"Tell me about it. But I need to get back for a meeting tomorrow with the Commander." Carlos had a feeling they were about to be given orders.

"Do you think you'll be headed to Portugal?"

It wasn't a surprise Ash asked about Portugal, considering it was all over the news. A bomb had gone off in the plaza in the center of Lisbon, killing four and injuring many others. ISIS had claimed responsibility. No doubt another team was already over there, but he wouldn't be surprised if they were going to be sent to provide back up or for a separate mission related to the people involved.

"I'm guessing that's likely. Listen, I need to know if you had any luck on getting some information I could use on Bryan Tosconi."

"Why?"

"I know he's just waiting for me to leave before he makes his next move on Erin. I need him out of the picture, pronto."

"Well, even if I did, it's going to be impossible to get him *out of the picture* by tomorrow."

Carlos sighed and ran a hand though his short hair. "Yeah, I know. Even if I can't get it done tomorrow, I'd still like to know there's something I can do." He relayed some information he'd kept from his friend. "He hit her, man. He's going to do it again, I know."

"Asshole. No one hits women."

"I could think of another name for him, but yeah, we protect women, not hit them." It sounded archaic to his ears, and he didn't mean that women were helpless. He had no doubt Erin could look after herself, but when it came to dealing with an angry man and his fists, usually no matter how savvy or smart a woman was, fists won out. And Bryan was bigger than Erin.

"Leave it with me, Italy. I'll see what I can find out. Plus I'll get someone to watch over Erin until we have this fucker behind bars."

His friend had answered the question he hadn't wanted to ask. "Thanks, man. I appreciate it."

They disconnected and Carlos sat back to sip his lukewarm coffee. It should make him feel better knowing Erin was going to be watched while he was away. Somehow it didn't though. There was still a part of him that didn't trust Bryan not to work out a way to evade whoever was watching Erin. The guard wasn't going to be sleeping in her house like Carlos had been.

No matter what he felt, come tomorrow morning he had to be on a plane to go back to his job and life. Only now he knew he'd be leaving a piece of himself here with Erin.

CHAPTER NINE

Having a bodyguard follow her every move seemed excessive to Erin. She'd argued with Carlos the last night they were together about it, telling him she didn't need anyone guarding her every damn minute every day of the week. She could look after herself, had been doing that a long time. Carlos had insisted that because Bryan was still lurking around, even though they hadn't seen him since the first night Carlos had followed her home, she needed to be protected.

The only good thing that came out of the argument was that they'd had incredible angry/make-up sex. A shiver of excitement shot through her body, pooling at the juncture between her thighs. She'd lost count of the orgasms he'd given her. Sleep had proven to be over-rated that night and, for the first time in her career, she'd closed her door at lunchtime and had a nap.

Now Carlos was away in God knows where, doing

God knows what, and she sat in her office trying to concentrate on work when all she wanted to do was speak to him.

Shit, she had it bad.

Her office phone rang and she grabbed it like a drowning person latching onto a life preserver. "Good morning, Erin Furlan speaking, how can I help you?"

Static. That's all she heard. Static. Fear gripped her. "Hello? Is anyone there?"

"Honey?"

"Carlos? Is that you?" Her heartbeat kicked up a notch and relief swept through her—it wasn't Bryan. From their conversations, she'd never expected he would call her. She was sure he said during missions he couldn't contact anyone.

Panic set in.

Was he hurt?

Was he in a situation where the likelihood of him returning was impossible?

Was this the last conversation they were ever going to have?

Erin pushed the thoughts out of her mind. Those kinds of ruminations weren't going to help her or help Carlos.

"Yeah, E, it's me. I wanted to let you know that I'm on my way back to the States. Can you come to Virginia for the weekend?"

Okay, this wasn't what she'd been expecting when she'd picked up the phone. But she would be lying to herself if she wasn't excited at the prospect of seeing Carlos.

"Yes. Yes, I can."

Static sounded the line again and Erin wasn't sure he heard her response.

"...bring ... if you want."

"What? You're breaking up."

"Sorry, honey, I'm on the plane and it's noisy as fuck. I said I'll email you my address and bring Antonia if you want."

Bring Antonia? Why would I do that?

"Why? I can travel by myself you know. I did tell you I lived in France for three years and travelled all around Europe, *by myself.*" The last thing she wanted was to be angry at the guy she hadn't seen or heard from in three weeks, but, dammit, his words annoyed the hell out of her. Plus, if he wanted her to bring Antonia, did that mean he didn't want to spend all the time they had together in bed? That was what she wanted to do.

He chuckled and her anger melted. She remembered what that chuckle felt like against her breast. As if her breasts remembered to, they hardened against her bra. "I know you can travel by yourself. Look, you don't have to bring her. I just thought you might like to."

"Oh no, you don't get off that easily Carlos Porcelli. There is a definite reason why you wanted me to ask Antonia, and if you don't tell me, then I won't come down, and you and your right hand can become very friendly over the weekend."

"Now that's just cruel, E."

"Cruel or not that could be your weekend. So spill, Porcelli."

"Fine. One of the guys saw the picture you sent me of the two of you together. He wants to meet her."

"Is he a good guy?"

"Who, Joker? Yeah he's a riot."

"*Joker?* His name is Joker?" No way was she going to set up her friend with a guy whose name was the same as an evil guy from a comic book series.

"No, that's his nickname. I want to see you, Erin. I missed you."

The last part was said so quietly she had to strain to hear it. "I missed you, too. And yes I'll come and bring Antonia. I can't wait to see you."

"Me either. I'll email you some details. Be careful, E."

The line cut out before she had a chance to respond. Thank goodness the call ended when it had. She had been on the verge telling Carlos she loved him.

Oh God, I love him.

I love him.

No, she couldn't. But it was true. She did. Had always loved him.

Oh boy, I am in so much trouble. During their week together, Carlos had told her how hard it was to have a relationship with someone. The lack of communication while he was away. The not knowing was the reason so many couples didn't make it.

Could she do it? Could she be in a loving relationship with Carlos and know that every time he went away he may not return to her?

Yes. Unequivocally yes.

If she only had six months with him, then it would be worth it. Over the last sixteen years she hadn't had a serious relationship, until she'd gotten involved with Bryan. She would've ended that relationship if she hadn't been so worried he would send some mob goons after her.

The only question was, how did Carlos feel about her?

He cared she knew that. If he didn't, he wouldn't have stuck around to guard her. Or arranged for someone to watch her while he was away. And not five minutes ago he'd told her he missed her.

Those things didn't add up to him loving her. She knew he hadn't seen his parents often after he'd been enlisted. A fact she knew broke his mother's heart. Did Carlos think by keeping his distance between him and those he loved, he was protecting them?

How wrong he was, and she was going to show him. She was going to show him that it was okay to love someone. Loving a person gave you strength. Love didn't diminish you.

While keeping her feelings hidden from him could prove difficult, she was going to do her best to convince him that letting her back into his life on a permanent basis, though risky, was the best type of risk he could take. As a Navy SEAL, didn't he take risks every day? The question was, was Carlos brave enough to risk his own heart? She planned to let him know it was the best risk he could take.

⸻

Carlos paced the arrival terminal waiting for Erin to walk through the glass sliding doors. He couldn't believe how nervous he was at seeing her again. While he'd been away, he'd spent half his time worrying about her safety and the other half worrying about his team's safety. He'd surprised himself when he needed to focus on their mission, he was able to push Erin to the back of his mind, and not let thoughts of her distract him like he had during their last mission.

Why was this time so different?

Was it because he'd spent time with her? Or was it because knowing she was back home—and how much he wanted to see her again—had sharpened his senses enabling him to sense danger before it happened so he could get back to her in one piece?

Was loving a person that much of an incentive to do his job right and get back home to her in one piece?

Love? Whoa, steady on sailor.

Carlos ignored that little voice, but couldn't tune it out.

Yes, he loved Erin. Loved her more than he thought possible. But did she love him, and was she willing to be a military wife?

He thought back to Wolf's team. All of them were married and had been for a while. They were a close unit and worked well together. They had each other's backs, like he and his team did, but there seemed to be something extra the melded that team together. Perhaps because they all knew they had family waiting for them, it drove them to be more diligent in their actions. He'd have to ask them when he saw them next. Whenever the hell that was going to be.

"Hey." A finger poked his chest, dragging him back from his thoughts.

Erin.

Acting purely on the love pulsating through his bloodstream, he latched an arm around Erin's waist and pulled her tight against him. With the accuracy of sniper's bullet, he zeroed in on her lips and captured them in a kiss.

The first touch and everything felt right in his world again. Fuck, he'd missed her so much. Her arms wrapped around his shoulders and her mouth opened, their tongues dueling. His spirits soared at her response. Could she have missed him too?

"It's. So. Good. To. See. You." He peppered each word with a kiss.

"Well, you're giving everyone quite the show. How about you two cool it?"

Sounds he'd blocked out returned. The buzz of conversations. Laughter. Phones chiming with messages or calls.

Carlos lifted his head and met Antonia's amused gaze. He lifted his chin. "Hey, glad you could make it."

"Well, don't expect me to give you that much of an

enthusiastic response to seeing you again," she responded drily.

Erin laughed in his arms before disentangling herself and looking at her friend. "I'm not going to apologize, Toni. I'm not ashamed."

He slung an arm around her, needing to keep her close. "Neither am I."

Antonia shook her head in disgust, but her smile said the complete opposite. "Let's get our bags. I hope I don't have to put up with this level of PDA all afternoon."

"Nah, we're heading to Robot's house. He's grilling. The whole team's going to be there."

"Robot?" Antonia asked as they headed to the baggage claim area.

"I'm guessing it's a nickname, right, babe?" Erin asked.

He squeezed Erin's shoulder, hearing her endearment for him on her lips again. "Yep."

Erin stopped suddenly and pulled out of his embrace. "Hey, I don't know your nickname? Why don't I know that?"

Carlos shook his head and grabbed her hand again. "It's nothing exciting. I don't want you to call me by my nickname. That would be too weird."

They reached the baggage carousels and waited to find out which one the girl's luggage would come out on.

"If I promise not to call you it, will you tell me?" Erin asked.

"It's not a big deal and well, if you want to call me by it, I don't mind."

"I'll decide when you tell me," Erin stated with her hands on her hips.

"Italy."

A little line appeared between Erin's eyes as she processed what he said. The moment she understood her eyes sparkled with amusement. "Ohh, well, that's original."

"It's rather boring isn't it," piped up Antonia. He raised an eyebrow at her. "Well, you know considering two of the other guys on your team are called *Joker* and *Robot*, Italy is kind of run of the mill. Can you change it?"

A buzzer sounded and an orange light flashed over a carousel. "Saved by arriving bags," he muttered and moved toward the revolving belt.

Twenty minutes later they were all in his SUV, heading toward Robot's house.

"You never did answer my question," Antonia commented after they'd hit the highway.

He glanced into the rearview mirror. "What question is that?"

"Can you change your nickname?"

"Nope, once you've got one, you've got one. And I don't want to change mine. I like it."

A warm hand landed on his thigh. "I like it too."

He placed one of his over hers. "Thanks, Honey."

"Ugh, you two are so sickening. Tell me again why I

agreed to come on this trip?" Antonia complained good-naturedly.

Erin laughed. "Two words—hot sailors."

"Eh, yeah, you're right."

Carlos laughed, enjoying the banter between them all. This was going to be a great weekend.

CHAPTER TEN

Erin had to admit, she was having a great time. Apprehension at meeting Carlos's team had rode her hard on the short plane trip from New York to Virginia. She'd been glad to have Antonia's company. She also understood why Carlos had suggested she bring her. Erin believed one of the guys on his team wanted to meet Antonia, in fact, Joker had pretty much pounced on her the second they'd walked through the side gate of Robot's back yard. Only Antonia had kept darting glances in their host's direction. That was interesting. She'd have to corner her friend when she got a chance.

"It can be a bit overwhelming, can't it?"

Erin whirled around to look at who'd spoken to her and found Caroline, Wolf's wife, standing behind her. "What can be?"

"All this testosterone congregated in a small area."

"You've got a point." Erin laughed and glanced

around the area. "How is it possible to have so many good-looking guys in one place?"

"Wait until you go to a bar which is full of them." Another woman joined their conversation. Erin recalled her name as Fiona. She was also married to a guy on Wolf's team.

"How do you do it?" Erin blurted out.

"Do what?" both women asked in unison.

"Be married to a guy who goes off and puts his life on the line constantly. How do you cope without having any contact with them? Not knowing whether they'll come back to you in one piece or not."

Caroline took her by the hand and headed over to a group of chairs that were vacant. Erin noticed her husband making a move to meet them, but backing away almost immediately at his wife's shake of her head.

Would she and Carlos ever be at the level of their relationship where they could communicate with just a look? She hoped they could.

A glass of wine was pushed into her hand as she sat in the chair. Erin smiled her thanks to Fiona. She took a sip of the white wine, welcoming the tartness of the liquid.

"Wine and ice-cream. Although I couldn't find any ice-cream," Fiona said.

It took a second for Erin to register what the other woman was saying. "You cope with your guys being away with wine and ice-cream?"

Caroline nodded. "Yep, and having noisy slumber parties where we all cry and get drunk."

Erin looked between the two women, convinced they were joking with her. Their expressions showed they weren't. "You're serious, aren't you?"

They both laughed. "Yep."

"Oh." Erin took another sip of her wine. Looking around the backyard, there were only four women: her, Antonia, Caroline and Fiona. None of the guys on Carlos's team were attached. She could see the other two women had a close friendship, like her and Antonia. She supposed she could share wine and ice-cream with Antonia. Her friend would be totally on board with that.

"You spend the whole time they're away crying and drunk?" Erin voiced her concern. While she liked the odd glass of wine, there was no way she was going become an alcoholic.

Shit, how many military wives were alcoholics?

"No." Caroline reached out and patted her hand on Erin's lap. "Some of us have jobs, and some of us have kids. It's only the first night we get messy. After that, we pull ourselves together and get on with things. But we spend as much time together when the guys are away on missions as possible. We usually always meet at my house."

Erin pondered over what the other women were saying as she scanned the crowd for Carlos, needing to see him to reassure herself that he was here and she wasn't dreaming.

There he was, standing by Robot, laughing at something his team lead said. He then turned his head and found her watching him. Her heart melted when he raised his fingers to his lips and blew her a kiss.

"Being the first is always the hardest."

"Pardon?" Erin asked and redirected her attention from her man to the women in front of her.

Caroline nodded. "Being the first woman to capture the heart of one of the team. Wolf and I were the first ones to fall in love. I was lonely when he went away, until one by one, the guys on the team found their women, and we became one big family who support each other with babysitting, shoulders to cry on, and giver of dirty looks when one of the guys messes up."

"Which isn't often, but when they do, they know they don't only have to answer to their wife. They have to answer to all of us," interjected Fiona.

"A family," Erin murmured.

"Yep. The best kind." Caroline clinked her wine glass with Fiona and then with Erin.

The chance to question the women further was lost when Carlos, Wolf, and another man walked over to them. Erin assumed it was Fiona's husband, Cookie, with the way the other woman's eyes went all dreamy and her body seemed to sway toward his when he squatted down and claimed her lips in a possessive kiss. When she looked over at Caroline she found Wolf was possessing her lips as well.

Now she knew how Antonia felt when she and Carlos had kissed at the airport. The sexual energy emanating from the other couples was intense.

"Do you think we should leave them?" Carlos whispered against her ear. Her breath caught in her throat and her nipples hardened against her bra.

"Or we could join them."

Images of them naked and arms wrapped around each other, fired through her brain. "I like the way you think."

Carlos lips connected with hers and soon she was lost in his kiss. If this was how it was going to be every time he returned home from being away, she wasn't going to complain. It was a pity that they still had the rest of the evening to get through before they could be alone.

Carlos unlocked the door of his apartment and flicked the light on. He scanned the room before allowing Erin to enter. It had been a great day and he couldn't wait to make it even better. It had been a surprise to see Wolf and Cookie at Robot's. It had given him a chance to talk to them about their relationships and how they kept their focus on the mission while they were away. The conversation had been enlightening and had given him hope that maybe he and Erin could make it work.

"Are you sure she's going to be okay?" Erin asked for the tenth time.

Carlos bit back a sigh. All he wanted to do was get Erin naked. He didn't want to discuss Antonia staying at

Robot's place. "Yes, she'll be fine. It's not like she's the only girl there. Fiona and Caroline will be there, too."

"Only until they leave, which I'm betting they've already done. Maybe I should call her."

"Robot will make sure nothing happens to her," Carlos said as he stopped her from reaching into her bag to get her phone out.

"Can you trust him?"

Exasperated, he blew out a breath to calm himself. "Honey, I trust *my life* with this man. He won't do anything or let anything happen to Antonia."

"You didn't see the looks she was sending him," muttered Erin.

The last thing he wanted to think about was Robot and Antonia. There was only one person he wanted to spend the rest of the night focusing on and that was the woman standing in front of him.

He took a few seconds to memorize what she was wearing and how she looked standing in his apartment. He'd never imagined she would be in his home. In her black capri pants, a soft pink t-shirt hugging her body, showing off her curves, she looked like she'd been made to fit him perfectly. Maybe she had.

He looped a tendril of her luscious brown hair behind her ear. "You have no idea how much I missed you."

Her face softened and a gentle smile tugged at her lips. "About as much as I missed you."

Carlos only had a second to brace as Erin launched

herself at him. He tightened his hold on her and captured her lips.

This.

This was what Wolf had been talking about that afternoon. The moment when you had your woman in your arms and everything was right in your world. You were invincible, because you knew the woman you held made you invincible. You were a better person because she was by your side.

Yes, life couldn't get much better than this. He had the woman he loved in his arms. A woman who'd slipped into his world seamlessly and now had gotten to know the other most important people in his life—his teammates.

Life was pretty damn good.

CHAPTER ELEVEN

"Well, this is a sucky way to end a great weekend." Erin lamented as the cab pulled out of Carlos's apartment complex. They'd been woken up by Carlos's phone ringing at too-early-o'clock. It had been fascinating to watch how he'd gone from being half asleep to combat ready alert in seconds. She'd known then he wouldn't be driving her to the airport, giving her one of those long passionate kisses goodbye you see in the movies when the heroine has to catch a plane.

She got the passionate kiss, just at his front door, not the airport gate. He'd given her a key and said it was hers to keep.

"I guess it's something you have to get used to if you stay with him," Antonio said.

"Yep." Even though she was scared, she knew that he would come home to her. He'd told her so. Plus, she'd met his team; they would all make sure they brought each other home—safely. "Did you enjoy your weekend, Toni?"

"Yeah, it was fine."

Erin flicked her gaze from out the window to Antonia. Her tone suggested her weekend was anything but fine. While Erin had spent quite a bit of time with Carlos, he'd made sure Antonia wasn't left out or ignored.

"What the hell?"

The cab driver's exclamation was the last thing she heard before the crunch of metal boomed around the car. She was jolted violently to the side and blackness engulfed her.

Slowly, the fog of darkness lightened and Erin reached out for it. Her eyelids fluttered open, before closing again at the bright light. Her head pounded and all she wanted to do was sink back into the darkness that beckoned her.

Part of her knew she couldn't though. Something had happened, but she couldn't remember. Maybe if she slept, thinking would be clearer when she woke up again.

"I know you're awake, bitch. Open your eyes or your friend gets hurt."

A ball of nausea bubbled up and she swallowed hard so she didn't spill the contents of her stomach on the ground. She knew that voice.

Bryan.

Everything came back to her then. She and Antonia had been headed to the airport when their cab had been hit. How the hell had Bryan known she was in Virginia? That she'd be traveling in a cab at that exact moment.

"Come on, Erin. I know you can hear me. If you don't open your eyes in the next five seconds, my friend here is going to make a pretty little cut on Antonia's face."

A whimper penetrated her fog and Erin fought to open her eyes. She couldn't let anything happen to her friend.

"Five, four, three."

With a strength of will, she raised her heavy eyelids. The room was blurry. She couldn't make out anything. Had no idea where Antonia was or how badly she was hurt.

"There's a good girl," Bryan mocked.

"You're a sick bastard." She blinked a few more times and slowly her vision cleared and the objects around the room stopped looking blurry. She was lying on a couch or a mattress. Being on her back put her at a disadvantage so she struggled to sit up and became aware that her hands and feet were bound together. Determined not to show any weakness in front of Bryan, she wiggled her legs to the ground, then pushed herself into a sitting position, her side screaming at the movement. She sucked in a breath, willing the pain away.

Her head swam and the nausea returned. Somehow

she managed to swallow it down—again. Bryan would take too much pleasure in seeing her toss her cookies.

Attempting to focus on her surroundings, she took in that they were in some sort of warehouse. The windows were grimy and the sunlight that tried to filter through cast eerie shadows around the room.

Antonia was seated in a chair opposite where Erin sat. Even with her spotty vision, it looked like Antonia was okay. There was blood on her top which Erin hoped came from glass and not a knife. From what she could remember, it was her side of the car that had taken the brunt of the accident.

"What do you want, Bryan?" The silence had stretched on for long enough. Fear threatened to engulf her. She wished Carlos was by her side. Although, if he had been, none of this would've happened.

How had it happened? Wasn't someone supposed to be watching her? Or did Carlos think because she was on his turf, with his team around, that Bryan wouldn't attempt anything.

He walked over to her, anger and hate filling his eyes. His lips turned up in a sneer. How had she ever thought him attractive? "I want what's mine, bitch."

A shudder ripped through her. Surely he wasn't talking about her. He didn't own her. Not now that she'd broken free of him. He didn't have the might of the Moretti Family behind him. No doubt he still knew some goons, but he didn't have the power to make her disappear.

Or did he?

The last thing she needed to do was to let that thought take over her mind. She had to believe he didn't.

"I don't know what you're talking about."

He slapped her across the face. Stars burst behind her eyes and the pounding in her head increased from a snare drum to a base drum.

"You are such a dumb fuck," he spat at her. "I know it was you who used my book to bring down *my* family. I don't know how you got the information, but you're going to pay for it. And your SEAL boyfriend isn't going to be able to do anything about it. I know he left today. I watched the two of you kissing at his door. Pathetic."

Her head injury must be more serious than she thought. He didn't just say he watched Carlos leave his apartment. Watched as they shared a kiss goodbye, did he?

"How?"

"You think I'm dumb. When you left New York, I knew it was my chance to strike."

A million thoughts ran through her mind. How had he known she was leaving New York? How had he tracked her so he could pounce when the moment struck?

"What would've happened if Carlos hadn't been called away?" Erin didn't think he had a hope in hell of snatching her if Carlos had been around.

"Doesn't matter, does it? He's gone and you're here. And he's never going to be able to locate you." He reached a hand toward her. Instinctively she flinched back. He laughed as he pressed a finger into her cheek. "You are never going to see him again."

No way would she believe that she was never going to see Carlos again. She looked over to Antonia. Her friend had tears streaming down her face. Antonia was the strongest person she knew, if she was crying then she had to be frightened for her own life.

No doubt Bryan had plans for her, but what plans did he have for Antonia? She didn't want to think about never seeing her best friend again. More than anything, they had to work out a way to get away from them. There was no chance in hell that she was going to be Bryan's victim.

Not anymore.

———

"What do you mean she didn't get on her flight?" Carlos gripped his phone tighter, willing Tex to tell him he was joking with him.

"Just that. Erin and Antonia never checked in. They never boarded. They never arrived in New York City."

This couldn't be happening. It had to be a bad dream. He was going to wake up any minute now and find himself back in his apartment with Erin curled around him.

Unfortunately, he was sitting at the base in San Diego waiting for their final orders. He couldn't go away if Erin was missing. It would be impossible for him to concentrate. Not only would he put himself at risk, he would be putting his team as well.

"You need to give me something here, Tex. Can you track her phone? Her credit card? Anything. What about Antonia, can you trace her as well?"

His voice rose and he drew the attention of his team. Robot walked over concern filling his gaze.

"I'm on it. I'll see what I can do. I'll get back to you."

Tex disconnected the call and Carlos stared at the screen. "Fuck."

"What's going on, Italy. Talk to me."

"Erin and Antonia are missing." God, even saying it out loud killed him. He met his team lead's and friend's eyes. "I can't go on this mission. I won't. I have to find them."

He strode past Robot, but his hand shot out and stopped Carlos's retreat. "Stop, Italy. You can't walk out of here. We've got orders, sailor."

"Let me go, Robot."

His arm was released and the need to walk out of the room faded a fraction. "This is my woman, Robot. She's missing. And I bet you my year's salary that it's that fucker, Bryan Tosconi, who's behind her disappearance."

His team lead nodded, understanding dawning. "Why do you say that?"

With his declaration, he'd basically told everyone on his team he was in love with Erin. Probably not a surprise to them, considering he hadn't been able to keep his hands off her at Robot's place. The admission left him vulnerable and that's the last thing he wanted. Carlos paced around the room, aware that the rest of the team's attention was focused solely on him. "Because it's the only thing that makes sense."

"Maybe they were in an accident and are at a hospital," Joker suggested.

An accident?

The thought hadn't crossed his mind, but if she'd been in an accident wouldn't she have been able to call him? Unless she was seriously hurt. Or worse. An icy chill swept over him at the thought of Erin lying on a cold metal table. "Fuck, Joker, you think that's better?"

Wolf strode through the door. "Tex called, he said your woman is missing. How can we help?"

The rest of Wolf's team filed into the room. The show of support from the other SEAL team was unexpected. Then again, after hearing the stories of how the other team had hooked up with their wives, he shouldn't have been surprised. Not that he could get them involved even though they offered. It wasn't a SEAL issue. This was a personal one. "Thanks for the offer, man. I only know what Tex has told me, and I'm going out of my fucking skin."

Wolf walked over and gripped his shoulder for a moment. "Tex will find her. He always does. Any ideas who may be behind this?"

"A guy who was a member of a mob family. One of our former teammates needed our help extracting his woman from her father, the head of one of New York's largest mob families. The Feds took down the family, but somehow this dickwad's lawyers got him out. He's been after Erin ever since."

"Why?" Abe asked.

"The information I gave to Ash and Tex to take down the Moretti family was given to me by Erin. And before you say anything, she's not part of the family."

Wolf watched him and his eyebrow rose, skepticism written all over his face. "Are you sure?"

Carlos clenched his fists. The question was a reasonable one to ask. Hell, he would ask the same thing if the roles were reversed. "Yes, I'm sure."

"What's going on here?" Commander Black's voice boomed around the room.

Carlos straightened up. "Nothing, sir."

"Somehow, I don't believe it." Their commander eyeballed them all. "Orders are in. You're wheels up in sixty minutes."

"I can't go, Sir."

"I don't think I heard you correctly, Porcelli. You don't get an option."

Tension swirled around the room. Without a doubt, his teammates were looking at him as if he'd taken a leave of his senses. What Wolf and his team thought of his stance he had no idea. They'd all been in a situation he now found himself in; the woman he loved was missing with no idea if she was alive or dead. He would be an anchor his team didn't need on this trip.

"I understand, Sir, but I have a personal issue that

I've just been made aware of. It would be a detriment to me and my team if I went on this mission."

He sensed his team closing around him. He appreciated the silent support of his brothers. Like on missions, they stood together as one.

"Sir." Robot stepped forward. "We believe Italy's girlfriend has been kidnapped."

"Believe? Is there a possibility she may have decided she didn't want to be with Italy?"

Someone snorted behind him, probably Joker. "If it was that, Sir, she would've got on her plane. But according to Tex, she and her friend Antonia didn't board their plane. And there's been no action on their credit cards to suggest they took an alternative method back to New York."

Commander Black tapped his chin, eyeing the other SEAL team in the room. "Why are you fellas here?"

"Tex informed us too, Sir." Wolf answered.

"We are talking former SEAL Tex Keegan?"

"Yes, Sir."

"Hmm. Okay." The Commander performed a military precision turn and stalked out of the room.

"What was that?" asked Joker.

"Hell if I know." Carlos pulled out his phone to see if Tex had called, texted or sent an email. That was stupid, considering he would've heard and felt it if the other man had done either of those things.

"You need a plan, Italy," Wolf started as the rest of his team congregated around them. "We can help with that, can't we?"

The rest of his team murmured their agreement. The offer was how SEAL teams worked. It didn't matter if they were SEAL team one or SEAL team six, they supported their brothers no matter what.

"'Preciate it, man."

"Now, before the Commander returns," Wolf started. "Let's go over what we know and see if we can come up with any other scenarios other than kidnapping."

Everything in Carlos hoped it wasn't a hostage scenario, but his itchy palm told him different.

CHAPTER TWELVE

G od, she was so thirsty and hungry. Erin had no idea how long they'd been shut up in the shitty warehouse. It had to have at least been a day. Bryan had disappeared hours ago, which surprised the heck out of her. She didn't think he'd want to leave her alone at all. The thought of escaping hadn't crossed her mind, because she knew her ex would have the place crawling with guys with big guns. She knew there was at least two guys in one of the rooms that overlooked the area where she and Antonia were.

There were no discernible sounds coming from outside. No birds or sounds of cars or trucks to give any indication of their location. At least Bryan had untied them and let Antonia move so they could sit together on the grimy couch.

"It's going to be all right, Toni." Once the words escaped her mouth, Erin didn't know if she'd said them to convince herself or Antonia.

"How can you say that? We've been stuck here for God knows how long now. No one even knows we're missing."

Nothing Antonia said wasn't true. She just hoped someone, somewhere had seen what had happened to them. Erin had no idea what Bryan had done with the cab driver. Maybe he was in on the scheme the whole time.

In her heart, she believed Carlos would come to her rescue. It didn't make sense for her to be so sure, but she was. He'd known how Bryan had hurt her. She hadn't breathed a word of it to him over the week they'd spent together, but he'd known. If, not *when*, they got out of this predicament she would ask him.

"I have to believe we're going to be fine, Toni. There's no other choice."

"I suppose you're thinking Carlos will ride in here on his white horse and save us?"

"Yes."

Antonia scoffed. "Jesus, Erin, this isn't a Disney movie where the handsome prince saves the day. This is real life."

Erin sighed. "Yes, I know. But if I give up hope, then Bryan wins, and he's won too many times in the past. He's not going to this time."

"I can't believe you let yourself get involved with someone who's tangled up in New York's mob scene, again."

"Again? What the hell are you talking about? When I started dating Bryan, I had no idea he was part of the

Moretti family. By the time I did, it was too late and when I tried to leave, well, let's just say he made it more than clear that leaving wasn't an option."

"I'm not talking about Bryan, we'll get back to him later. I'm talking about Carlos."

"Carlos? He hasn't been around for sixteen years. How could he be involved with the mob?" Erin was beginning to think Antonia had suffered a head injury in the accident. That was the only reasonable explanation for suggesting Carlos had been mixed up with the mob. The man was a SEAL for heaven's sake.

"You were so star struck by him in high school you had no idea he was a runner for the Forlani family."

"No, that's not true," she whispered. It couldn't possibly be true, could it? Why would Antonia lie to her? They'd been best friends since first grade. If there was one person she could always count on, it was Antonia.

"It is. I'm sorry, Erin. I don't know how he managed to keep it from you. Part of me admires him for being able to keep that side of himself hidden. But the other part hates that he did this to you."

Erin closed in on herself, attempting to process all her best friend told her. Slowly, she allowed her mind to go back over their time in high school. The times when Carlos would not be able to meet her after school like they'd plan. The times he missed classes. She'd put it down to him being a typical teenage boy who didn't want to be in school.

A particular time stuck out in her mind, when he'd

turned up at school with a black eye and when she'd tried to hug him, he'd winced. He'd passed it off as he and his brother roughhousing at home and he'd fallen down the stairs. Now, after being on the receiving end of a mob beating, it was obvious he'd done something he shouldn't have.

"Fuck, I was such a fool. And I helped that idiot with giving him information to bring down the Moretti family. I should've let him meet up with Rico instead of saying I'd help him."

"Why did you help him?" Antonia asked.

"Because he's a SEAL and I thought he could help me. I wanted to get away from Bryan. For a short while I had my freedom." Now she found herself kidnapped, locked up in some warehouse, and found out the guy she'd fallen in love with not once, but twice, had been involved with the mob as well. "Shit, I've got a type."

Antonia chuckled beside her. "Nah, not really."

Silence descended around them again and fatigue bit at her heels. She'd only allowed herself to doze, not wanting to give Bryan or his goons any reason to hurt her or Antonia. Well, hurt them more than they'd done. Plus, she knew she had a concussion so sleeping could be dangerous for her.

"I'm so tired," she muttered.

Antonia grabbed her hand and moved so she was comforting her. "Rest, I'll keep an eye out."

Erin squeezed her friend's hand. Maybe she would close her eyes for a few minutes. "I'm sorry, Toni."

"What for?"

"Getting you in this mess. Making you come on this trip with me. If you hadn't you'd be safe in New York." Guilt plagued Erin with every passing second they were stuck in this situation.

"If I wasn't here, you'd be alone. And that would be even worse. Besides," she paused. "Who would complain about spending the weekend being surrounded by so many hot SEALs?"

Erin laughed, pleased that Antonia could see something light in their horrible situation. "This is true. Did you spend much time with Joker?" If Antonia hadn't been so close, Erin would've missed the slight tensing of her body.

"Uh, no. Um not really."

Pop. Pop. Pop.

All thoughts of picking apart her friend's response to her question flew out of her mind.

"What was that?" Antonia asked.

"I'm not su—" At the sound of some yelling, the guys who had been sitting in the room, watching them, burst out of it and ran down a hallway. "Toni, move. Get behind the couch."

Pain screamed through her head and side at her sudden movement. She didn't care. The only thing she was concentrating on was finding somewhere safe to hide.

Once they were safely behind the couch, Erin's heartbeat slowed down a fraction. After the initial sound that spurred them all into action, there'd been nothing but silence. That couldn't be good.

"What do you think's happening?" asked Antonia.

"No idea."

"Do you think it could be someone coming to rescue us?"

How Erin wanted to believe it would be Carlos and his team rescuing her. No matter how impossible that could be. The guy was probably in the middle of some war-torn country saving people in more danger than her. "Could be. Or it could be someone after Bryan. I have a feeling he's less than subtle in his dealings."

It amazed Erin at how calm she sounded. Shouldn't she be panicking? Hell could be about rain down on them, yet she was talking to Antonia as if they were sharing a coffee.

A window shattered somewhere to their right and smoke seeped toward them. Any bravery she had disappeared at the sight of the grey mist stretching its way across the room. With a quick look over her shoulder, Erin could see their chance of escaping the area was limited. She prayed that whoever had thrown the gas canister was there to help them, not kill them.

Erin screamed as her arm was grabbed and she was yanked upright. Bryan had returned. Where had he been and why hadn't he run out of the building with his two goons?

"Leave her alone," Antonia screeched and punched Bryan's arm.

"Shut up," Bryan responded as he raised the arm holding a gun and cracked the handle against Antonia's head. Her friend crumpled in a heap, red dripping down her face.

"Oh my God, Toni." She attempted to pull away, but Bryan wouldn't let her. "You've killed her." Life without having her childhood best friend wasn't something she wanted to face.

"Knocked out. If I wanted to kill her, I'd have shot her." He shoved her forward, away from the safety of the couch. "You're my insurance, bitch."

He held the gun to her temple and marched her toward the middle of the room. With a last glance over her shoulder, she prayed that Antonia was going to be okay and prepared to meet her fate.

Whatever it may be.

CHAPTER THIRTEEN

The second he'd received the text from Tex advising that he'd located Erin and Antonia, adrenaline spiked through Carlos's blood like it did whenever they went out on assignment. The fact this assignment was extremely personal to him, heightened his need to jump into action without thinking first. Fortunately for him, he had his team at his back who knew what was at stake and pulled him back from creating an even bigger mess.

"Easy, Italy," Robot's voice sounded in his ear. "Wolf and his team haven't given the signal yet. We wait."

Carlos knew the plan. They'd gone over it numerous times on the flight from California to Virginia. They'd gone over other plans, too. In their game nothing was ever straight in or out. They made contingency plans. And then made contingency plans for contingency plans. Tex had eyes on the warehouse where Bryan had taken the girls and kept them updated on any movements.

When Commander Black had walked back into the room where his team and Wolf's team were situated, Carlos had fully expected to be told if he went against orders he'd be spending time with the military police. Instead, his Commander had announced that another team would be taking their mission and the two teams in the room would be used to rescue Erin and Antonia.

Once the shock had worn off, he questioned Wolf about why the change in plans. His explanation had involved one word. *Tex.* When he'd gone to ask the other man more questions, he'd held up his hand in a clear sign that the less Carlos asked the better.

The how's and why's didn't matter. All that mattered was they were now standing outside the warehouse that housed the woman he loved and her best friend. It dawned on Carlos that Tex looked like he had clearance that even superseded their Commander's, if he could work it so the team didn't have to leave and Wolf's could join them on this unsanctioned mission, what else could the other man do? Commander Black's instructions had been implicit—get in, get out, with no deaths. Tex advised once they were clear, he'd get the Feds on the scene to clean up the mess.

"Alpha one, perimeter secure." Abe's voice crackled through his earpiece and Carlos's adrenaline ratcheted up to hyper level.

This was it.

Erin was inside. He was seconds away from clapping his eyes on her again. It would take everything in him not to pull the trigger and blow Bryan's brains out. But he was a SEAL, and he followed orders—no matter what.

"On my command," Robot said. "Italy, whatever you see, control your fucking self. Remember no deaths."

"I know."

They used the late afternoon shadows to mask their movements as they crept along the side of the building, their trust that Wolf's team had disarmed and rendered the guys patrolling the outside of the building, absolute. No way would the other team let them in if it wasn't.

Robot held up his fist and they halted. He gave directions for Joker and Cowboy to remain where they were to keep watch. He then directed Red and T-Rex to take the left side of the building.

Carlos wasn't surprised to find himself paired with his team lead. If the roles were reversed, he'd do the same. He used the few moments it took for Red and T-Rex to throw the smoke canister to center himself. Two deep breaths and his usual calmness washed over him. He wasn't going to let Erin down.

Robot nudged his shoulder. This was it. He grabbed the flash bombs and lowered his protective eyewear. He mentally counted down from five and together he and Robot stormed through the front door, tossing flash grenades as they went.

He heard the distinctive sound of a feminine scream.
Erin.

"Steady, Italy."

"I'm fine," he ground the words out. "Can you make out the girls?"

"Negative, but the scream came from the left."

He and Robot moved in that direction. T-Rex and Red reported they were coming from the right.

A shot sounded in the air, and he and Robot stopped.

"Don't move any further, you fuckers, especially you *Carlos*, otherwise the next bullet won't be in the air."

"That asshole," Carlos hissed out as he and Robot began their stalking again. "Anyone got visual?" he asked.

"He's in the middle of the room, gun to Erin's temple." T-Rex reported.

"I've got a clear maim shot," Cookie's voice sounded over the radio.

Carlos wanted to be the one who took out Bryan, but at this minute he didn't care. All he wanted was to get Erin out safely.

"Any eyes on the second female, Antonia?" asked Robot.

"Nega-wait," Red said. "Down behind the couch in the left-hand corner of the room, there's a form on the ground. Unable to determine if she's injured or not. She's not moving."

If Antonia was dead, Carlos would never forgive himself. He'd been the one to suggest Erin bring her along.

"Take him out," Robot's steely voice resounded in his ear.

A shot echoed around the warehouse, followed by a scream then another shot.

"Who fired the second shot?" Carlos shouted. A chorus of *negatives* pounded his earpiece. "Shit. Confirm mark is down. Confirm mark is down."

"Affirmative," replied Cookie.

Carlos slung his gun over his shoulder and ran toward the center of the room. Robot was on his heels. He noticed instead of following him, his team lead veered off to where Red had indicated Antonia was located. He skidded to a halt, his breath in his throat when he spied Erin crumpled on the floor, blood pooling around her. Bryan lay beside her, gripping his knee and howling like a baby. If Carlos wasn't under a *no kill* order, he'd put a bullet between Bryan's eyes to shut him the fuck up.

He kicked the other man's gun out of the way and crouched down beside Erin. The man inside him fought against the sailor. The sailor won out and instead of scooping Erin up and clutching her close, he took the time needed to locate where the blood was coming from. She had a bullet wound to the upper arm. Not a serious wound, certainly wouldn't explain why she was unconscious.

Running his hands around and underneath her head he encountered the telltale stickiness of blood.

"Erin's been shot and has a head wound. Are medics on the way?" he asked

"Bitch, deserves to be hurt. She took away my livelihood." Bryan tried to reach out toward Erin, but T-Rex and Red were there in seconds dragging the injured man away.

"Buddy, where you're going, I guarantee you'll be someone's bitch." Red taunted. "Italy, medics five minutes out. Wolf and his team are rounding up the guys they disabled around the perimeter. Feds will be here shortly."

Carlos maneuvered himself so that Erin's head rested on his lap. Leaning forward he kissed her on the forehead. "Help is on the way, honey. Hang on." He took a deep breath, ready to utter the words he hadn't spoken to any other woman apart from Erin and his mom. "I love you, Erin. I never stopped."

A thick, dark fog enveloped Erin again. It took an effort she wasn't sure she possessed to lift her eyelids. Her head thumped, and a million little drummer boys playing out a beat she had no desire to dance to. Over the drumming, she could make out the consistent *beep beep* of a monitor. Like the ones she'd seen in all the hospital dramas she watched.

A hospital. I'm free.

In between the veil of total unconsciousness and wide awake, all the events leading up to this moment coalesced in her mind.

The cab being hit.

Bryan kidnapping her and Antonia.

Being left tied up in a warehouse.

Gunshots and then a grey smoke that burned her eyes.

The vague outline of SEALs filing into the room.

Then pain. Red-hot pain in her arm, before falling and cracking her head again.

A faint memory stirred beneath the images of her ordeal.

I love you, Erin. I always have.

Had Carlos really spoken those words to her, or were they a wishful dream, conjured up during a situation where she had no idea if she'd survive or not?

A soft sound broke up the monotonous beeping machine. A sound like boots hitting the ground. She inhaled deeply, assaulted by the pungent smell of antiseptic synonymous to hospitals, but there, beneath it a glimmer of citrus.

Carlos.

"Erin? Honey?" Clothes rustled and her hand was engulfed by a warm one. While another one cupped her cheek. "Open your eyes, E, please."

It took a couple of tries, but she managed to get her lids lifted. The harsh light pierced her brain. The drummers in her head took it as a sign to up their tempo. She slammed them down again. Head injuries sucked. She never wanted to experience another one again.

"Hurts," she whispered.

"I know, honey. You've got a severe concussion. Not to mention a bullet wound to your upper arm."

Now that he mentioned it, pain radiated down her arm. While her attention had been centered on her head, it had blocked out the ache in her arm.

"Will match you." Her lips and throat were parched, making it impossible to string a sentence together. A plastic straw brushed against her mouth. She took a couple of swallows, enjoying the slide of the liquid down her throat. She went to take more but the cup was pulled away.

"No, you shouldn't drink too much. Now try opening your eyes again. It won't hurt this time."

"Promise?" He chuckled, the sound sending delicious tremors of delight down her spine. How could she be lying in bed injured, with her eyes closed, and get aroused by a small laugh? Her body needed to concentrate on helping her cope with pain, not reacting to every little thing Carlos did.

"I can't promise it won't hurt, but maybe not as much."

How she wanted to see the man who said he loved her. Yes, she believed it wasn't a conjuring of her imagination, but the truth. This time when she opened her eyes the pain, while intense, was bearable.

"There you are."

Her vision filled with Carlos's face. "There you are," she responded.

"Yes." He lowered his head and brushed his lips softly over hers. "I'm sorry, E. I'm sorry this happened to you. I should've made sure you and Antonia were safe before I left."

"Antonia! Oh my God, Antonia. Is she okay?"

"Honey, she's fine. Sporting a sore head like you, but that's all."

Relief coursed through her, knowing her best friend was fine. "Where is she? When can I see her? I need to see her."

"Hey, calm down." He scooped her into his arms and a she melted against him. "She's fine, down the hall in another room. Last I knew, Robot was with her."

"Robot? Not Joker?" The whole reason Antonia had come on the trip that had ended with their capture was because Joker wanted to meet her. She hadn't had a chance to ask her friend about her hooking up with Robot. That is if they did hook up. They would need to have a serious talk the moment they got out of hospital.

"Yeah, I don't know what happened, but Robot rode in the ambulance with Antonia. But don't feel bad for Joker, he was making friendly with a nurse the moment we arrived."

"Everyone is here?" Her befuddled mind was trying to process what Carlos was saying, but she had to admit she was having some difficulty.

"Yep, all the guys wanted to make sure you and Antonia were all right. Wolf's team is here as well."

So much information her bruised mind couldn't take it all in. Her eyes drifted shut. It took too much energy to keep them open. Before she could let herself sleep she needed to know something else. "Bryan?"

"Never going to hurt you again. Sleep, E. You're safe now."

She wanted to believe Carlos and had no reason to doubt him, but she wouldn't relax until she could see for herself that he wouldn't be getting free again and her life was her own. A life she wanted to share with the man sitting on the bed next to her. Question was, did he want to be a part of her life?

The next time she woke, her brain had stopped pounding and her arm no longer ached. The monitor still echoed around the area. A nightlight glowed around the room. She was alone on the bed now. A look to her left and she found Carlos sprawled out on a chair, legs straight out, arms crossed against his chest and his head lolling to the side. It looked about as comfortable as sleeping on a bed of rocks, and she wouldn't be surprised if he had in fact slept on rocks at some stage of his life.

The soft light casting shadows over him only high-lighted how handsome and strong he was. The beard covering his jaw was thicker than when he'd first appeared in New York. It seemed like a lifetime ago, but was mere weeks.

How much had her life changed in that time?

How important this man sleeping on the chair had come to mean to her. She loved him and she wanted to spend her life with him. But he'd told her it would take a special woman to be the wife of a Navy SEAL. Did she have it in her to handle when he went away at a moment's notice? To handle not knowing if he would return to her.

Yes.

An unequivocal yes. Life without Carlos in it wasn't worth thinking about. If she only had him for a short time then that would be that, but to not have him at all wasn't something worth thinking about.

She recalled Antonia's words about Carlos's past association with a mob family. Yes, it was wrong of him to keep it from her. But he'd shielded her from his association. She understood even more his desire to enlist. It had been his way of escaping a life that could've been detrimental to him. She wasn't going to let it slide. She would bring it up with him, but it wasn't going to stop her from wanting a future with him.

A warm hand closed over hers making her jump at the contact. "You're thinking awfully hard."

"I love you." *Shit I wasn't going to say that.* How could she have just vomited that phrase out? Way to scare the guy away.

A second later a strong, heavy SEAL landed on her bed, his hands framed her face. "E," he whispered. "God, you slay me."

He lowered his head and kissed her, his lips moving softly over hers. She didn't know what to make of his words, but his kiss was telling her he cared. Her arms crept around him clutching at his back, keeping him close to her.

The heart monitor picked up pace, the beeping sound becoming erratic. The door flung open and a nurse rushed into the room. "Is everythin…Right okay." She backed out of the room before Erin could comprehend the interruption.

Carlos pulled his lips away, chuckling. "Guess this isn't the place to have a make out session when hooked up to machines."

Mortification at the words she'd blurted out and having a nurse interrupt them, she attempted to lie back down. Carlos's arms tightened around her. "Not so fast."

"I'm sorry," she whispered.

"Sorry for what?" His hand drew lazy circles down her back, frying her already frazzled senses even more.

"I shouldn't have said what I said."

"Said what?" His eyebrow lifted in question and she knew he was being deliberately obtuse. He was trying to make her say it again. She lifted her eyes to stare into his glittering brown ones. They were open wide, showing her exactly what his was feeling. It gave her the strength to say the words again.

"I love you, Carlos *Italy* Porcelli."

A smile she hadn't seen in sixteen years stretched his lip wide. "Thank God, because I love you too, E. I love you so much. But I'm so scared."

Her heart melted as her big, brave Navy SEAL shared his vulnerability with her. She knew his fears. She shared them. "Me too, but together we're brave enough and strong enough to battle through anything. Because we have each other and will be each other's pillar of steel when needed."

"You are amazing, you know that?"

"I'm far from amazing, but I'll take it."

Carlos gathered her close and she snuggled into her man. "We've got a lot to work out, E. Your job, my job."

"Your past," she interjected, and immediately wanted to snatch it back.

"My past?"

"Yes. I know about your past with the Forlani family. I know you worked for the mob."

The man holding her tensed like an iron bar beside her. "How did you find out?"

"Antonia."

"Right." A breath whooshed out of him. "I'm sorry, I should've said something during the week we spent together in New York. It was wrong of me to keep it from you."

She reached up and touched his cheek. "I understand, Carlos. I could be a bitch about it, demanding an explanation. But after what I've been through in the last two days, wondering if I'd ever get to see you again, getting worked up over something that happened so many years ago isn't worth it."

His lips brushed hers. "I don't deserve you," he whispered.

"No, you don't, but you're stuck with me, Italy."

He chuckled before he turned serious again. "Unfortunately, it's not quite over yet."

"What do you mean?"

"There's still the fallout from the situation with Bryan to deal with."

She shuddered in his arms knowing he was right. She may feel wonderful now, even with the aching head and arm, but she wasn't going to always be this way. No doubt she would be questioned about Bryan and the kidnapping and the information she'd shared with Carlos all those months ago and how she found it. "I know. And whatever will happen, we will face it together, because neither one of us alone now."

"Damn right. We've got each other. Welcome to my team, Erin Furlan."

"I *love* being a member of your team, Carlos."

CHAPTER FOURTEEN

Once again they were all in Robot's backyard enjoying an afternoon grilling session. Wolf's team and their wives had also joined them. Even Antonia was there, having made the trip down from New York for the weekend. She was doing everything possible to avoid their host. An interesting situation and one Erin still needed to get to the bottom of. Her best friend was being very closed mouth about her and Robot.

So much had happened in the last two months since her kidnapping. She'd been questioned by the Feds and helped them with putting Bryan away, for a long time this time. Once it was all over Carlos had asked her to come live with him in Virginia. Being apart from her man wasn't an option, so she'd handed in her resignation. With her credentials, she'd been able to secure another GM job at hotel, this time with a big chain. The best part was being able to come home to her man every night he was in town.

"Hey, Erin, how ya doing?"

Erin looked up and saw Caroline and Summer standing in front of her. She couldn't believe how close she'd become to the wives of Wolf's team. Maybe because they'd all experienced something similar to her.

"Great, thanks." She pointed to the vacant chairs beside her. "Come sit."

The other women sat down, and Maria—Riley's girlfriend the one who started the journey for her and Carlos's reunion—joined them as well. "Can I sit, too?" she asked.

"Sure," Erin said. "The more the merrier."

"Ugh, don't say that, then everyone will want to party with us," Caroline groaned and laughed at the same time.

Erin laughed too. "Come on, Caroline I happen to know you love these get togethers. I have it on good authority you and Wolf are always throwing one at your place."

"She's got you there," Summer piped up.

Caroline threw her hands in the air. "True and what can I say, I love my SEAL and I love my SEAL family."

"I'm beginning to feel the same way. Although," Erin murmured and looked over at Maria. They may live in New York and her man may be a retired SEAL, but once a SEAL always a SEAL so she considered them her family, too. "We don't have the same numbers as you. It's only Maria and me."

"Don't forget Lily, even though we can't be here often," Maria inserted.

"Well you know if you need us we're a Skype call way."

Erin knew this. In fact, she and Caroline had shared many phone calls dealing with the aftermath of Bryan taking her. She'd been able to express herself to the other woman in a way Caroline understood and she'd helped Erin cope with her nightmares and fears. Of course, Carlos had been with her every step of the way, but sometimes a woman's rational and logic was needed.

"Should I be worried? You're not trying to scare my woman away, are you?" Carlos's hand landed on her shoulder and she automatically placed her hand over his.

"Nope, you're stuck with me."

"Good. I like being stuck with you."

Caroline and the other women stood. "I think that's our cue to leave. We'll catch up later on, Erin."

"Sounds good to me." She didn't see the other women leave, her attention solely on Carlos who now squatted in front of her.

"You having a good time, E?" he asked, his tone serious. She could tell it was important to him that she enjoy this down time with his team. They were more his family than his brother and parents. Each man standing in this yard laid their life on the line every mission or each other.

"The best. I love you, *Italy*," she teased him, knowing he liked it when she called him by his real name. She didn't mind as to her he was always Carlos and not Italy.

"You're going to pay for that, later."

Her body shuddered at the method of payment he was going to extract from her. "I can't wait."

"I think I should come up with a nickname for you," he said as he stood and pulled her up into his arms.

She automatically wound hers around his neck. "Is that right? So *Honey* and *E*, aren't nicknames?"

"Sure, but I think you need a special one."

"I don't need a special nickname, Carlos. I just need you."

He kissed her softly on her lips before pulling away and brushing his thumb across her cheek. "You have me, *Honey E,* now and forever."

I f you enjoyed this book please consider leaving a review. All reviews are greatly appreciated.

JOIN my Newsletter and find out about sales, free books, contests and new releases before anyone else!! Click HERE

ACKNOWLEDGMENTS

I want to say a big thank you to Susan Stoker for opening up her world to me again. I had a great time the first time and couldn't wait to visit again. Also to her readers who welcomed me and my books with open arms. I hope you enjoy Erin and Carlos's story.

To my beta's Abigail Owen and Wren Michaels, thanks for your insight and help in making this book to be even better.

Erin Fehres, thanks for allowing me to use your name for this book. Thanks also for helping us out when we needed it.

My beautiful cover was, once again, created by Jennifer from More Than Words Promotions. Your continued support and friendship is greatly appreciated.

To my family, my loves, this has been a trying couple of months. Thank you for helping me through my injury.

ABOUT THE AUTHOR

On her very first school report her teacher said 'Nicole likes to tell her own stories'. Many years later she eventually sat down and wrote her first book.

Nicole writes sexy contemporary romances, seducing you one kiss at a time as you turn the pages. She enjoys taking two characters and creating unique situations for them.

Learn more about Nicole Flockton at http://www.nicoleflockton.com.

authornicole@nicoleflockton.com

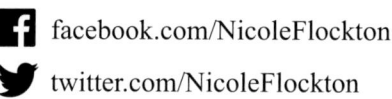 facebook.com/NicoleFlockton
twitter.com/NicoleFlockton

ALSO BY NICOLE FLOCKTON

Guardian Seals Series

Protecting Lily

Protecting Maria

Guarding Erin

Guarding Suzie

Guarding Brielle

The Elite

Fighting to Win

Fighting to Dream

Fighting for Love

Fighting for Redemption

The Freemasons

The Victor

The Hunter

Sweet Texas Secrets

Sweet Texas Fire

Sweet Texas Series Boxed Set

Bound Series

Bound by Her Ring

Bound by His Desire

Bound by Their Love

Bound by The Billionaire's Desire - Boxed Set

Lovers Unmasked Series

Lovers Unmasked: The Complete Series

Masquerade

Rescuing Dawn

Seducing Phoebe

Emerald Springs Legacy Series

Daniel's Decision

Emerald Springs Legacy Collection

Standalone Titles

White Knight (Co-Written with Abigail Owen)

Novellas

Tangled Vines

Melt My Heart Anthology

Tango Love

A Vacation Affair

Medal Up: A Winter Games Duology

Swipe for Mr. Right

Wrong Time for Mr. Right

As you know, this book included at least one character from Susan Stoker's books. To check out more, see below.

Delta Force Heroes Series

Rescuing Rayne (FREE!)
Rescuing Aimee (novella)
Rescuing Emily
Rescuing Harley
Marrying Emily
Rescuing Kassie
Rescuing Bryn
Rescuing Casey
Rescuing Sadie
Rescuing Wendy
Rescuing Mary (Oct 2018)
Rescuing Macie (April 2019)

Badge of Honor: Texas Heroes Series

Justice for Mackenzie (FREE!)
Justice for Mickie
Justice for Corrie
Justice for Laine (novella)
Shelter for Elizabeth
Justice for Boone
Shelter for Adeline
Shelter for Sophie
Justice for Erin
Justice for Milena

Shelter for Blythe
Justice for Hope (Sept 2018)
Shelter for Quinn (Feb 2019)
Shelter for Koren (June 2019)
Shelter for Penelope (Oct 2019)

SEAL of Protection Series
Protecting Caroline (FREE!)
Protecting Alabama
Protecting Fiona
Marrying Caroline (novella)
Protecting Summer
Protecting Cheyenne
Protecting Jessyka
Protecting Julie (novella)
Protecting Melody
Protecting the Future
Protecting Kiera (novella)
Protecting Dakota

SEAL of Protection: Legacy Series
Securing Caite (Jan 2019)
Securing Sidney (May 2019)
Securing Piper (Sept 2019)
Securing Zoey (TBA)
Securing Avery (TBA)
Securing Kalee (TBA)

New York Times, *USA Today* and *Wall Street Journal*
Bestselling Author Susan Stoker has a heart as big as

the state of Texas where she lives, but this all American girl has also spent the last fourteen years living in Missouri, California, Colorado, and Indiana. She's married to a retired Army man who now gets to follow *her* around the country.

She debuted her first series in 2014 and quickly followed that up with the SEAL of Protection Series, which solidified her love of writing and creating stories readers can get lost in.

If you enjoyed this book, or any book, please consider leaving a review. It's appreciated by authors more than you'll know.

www.stokeraces.com
www.AcesPress.com
susan@stokeraces.com

Nicole Flockton: Protecting Maria
Nicole Flockton: Guarding Erin
Nicole Flockton: Guarding Suzie
Nicole Flockton: Guarding Brielle
Casey Hagen: Shielding Nebraska
Casey Hagen: Shielding Harlow
Casey Hagen: Shielding Josie
Desiree Holt: Protecting Maddie
Kathy Ivan: Saving Sarah
Kathy Ivan: Saving Savannah
Kathy Ivan: Saving Stephanie
Jesse Jacobson: Protecting Honor
Jesse Jacobson: Fighting for Honor
Jesse Jacobson: Defending Honor
Jesse Jacobson: Summer Breeze
Silver James: Rescue Moon
Silver James: SEAL Moon
Silver James: Assassin's Moon
Becca Jameson: Saving Sofia
Kate Kinsley: Protecting Ava
Heather Long: Securing Arizona
Heather Long: Guarding Gertrude
Heather Long: Protecting Pilar
Heather Long: Covering Coco
Kirsten Lynn: Joining Forces for Jesse
Margaret Madigan: Bang for the Buck
Margaret Madigan: Buck the System
Margaret Madigan: Jungle Buck
Margaret Madigan: December Chill
Rachel McNeely: The SEAL's Surprise Baby

Made in United States
Cleveland, OH
30 November 2025

27023459R00098